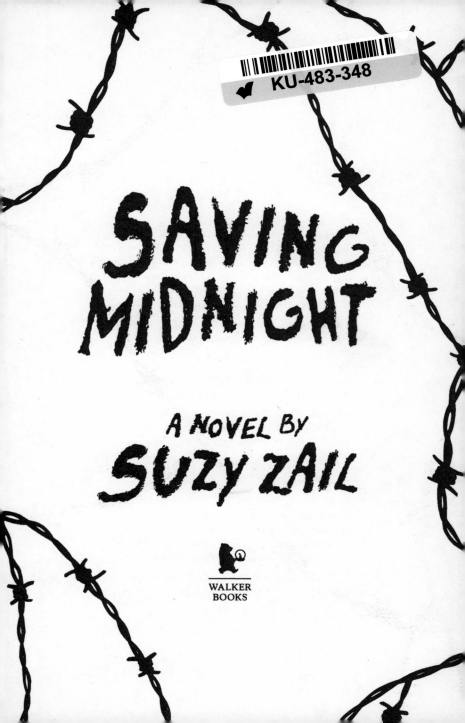

KU-483-348

SAVING MIDNIGHT

A NOVEL BY SUZY ZAIL

WALKER
BOOKS

This is a work of fiction. Names, characters, places and incidents
are either the product of the author's imagination or, if real, used
fictitiously. All statements, activities, stunts, descriptions, information
and material of any other kind contained herein are included for
entertainment purposes only and should not be relied on for
accuracy or replicated as they may result in injury.

First published in Great Britain 2015 by Walker Books Ltd
87 Vauxhall Walk, London SE11 5HJ

2 4 6 8 10 9 7 5 3 1

Text © 2014 by Suzy Zail
Cover photograph © 2015 Leighanne Payne/Getty Images

The right of Suzy Zail to be identified as author of this
work has been asserted by her in accordance with the
Copyright, Designs and Patents Act 1988

This book has been typeset in Bembo

Printed and bound in Great Britain by Clays Ltd, St Ives plc

All rights reserved. No part of this book may be reproduced,
transmitted or stored in an information retrieval system in any
form or by any means, graphic, electronic or mechanical,
including photocopying, taping and recording, without prior
written permission from the publisher.

British Library Cataloguing in Publication Data:
a catalogue record for this book is available from the British Library

ISBN 978-1-4063-5784-4

www.walker.co.uk

For Fred Steiner, A10567

Chapter 1

Alexander Altmann stood in the dusty grey square, sweating. He looked up at the sun and guessed it was midday. His stomach growled. If he was home, his mother would be calling him to come in for lunch. He felt his eyes start to well. "Stop it," he said under his breath. "Stop feeling sorry for yourself." He wiped his nose on his sleeve and waited for his number to be called. He didn't need to look down at his arm at the number tattooed onto his skin. He knew it by heart. A10567.

The last time he'd heard his name was five weeks ago, maybe six. He hadn't recognized his mother when she'd called out to him. Her head had been shaved and she wore mismatched shoes and a tattered dress that gaped at the neck and, for the first time since he'd stepped off the train, Alexander realized what he must look like.

"Alex!" she'd cried, clinging to the barbed

wire fence that separated the men's camp from the women's barracks. "Alex! It's me." They'd fed their fingers through the gaps in the wire and Alexander remembered feeling elated, and then sick to the stomach when he realized his sister wasn't with her.

He tried to banish the memory and make his mind go blank. He was used to blue skies and green fields, to nickering horses and the sound of the wind rustling the leaves. Not the sound of guns. He listened for the whistling wind and the buzz of insects, but when he opened his eyes the sky above Birkenau was still dirty with smoke and all he could hear was the brutal sound of men shouting and dogs barking.

"Caps off!" An SS guard drew a rubber baton from his belt. Alexander pulled his cap from his head and cursed silently.

"Caps on!"

Alexander set the blue and white cap back on his head and grumbled to himself. *What was the point of having prisoners do endless drills that sapped their energy?* Then a boy, two rows up, collapsed and Alexander realized – that was the point.

"Caps off." The guard stopped before an old man clutching his stomach. "Caps off!" he shouted, spit gathering at the corners of his mouth. The man raised a birdlike arm but the guard was faster, knocking the old man's striped cap from his head. Alexander watched the man stoop to pick it up and saw the guard smile and reach for his gun. Alexander clenched his fists and dug his nails into the soft skin of his palms until the pain blunted all thought. The first time he'd seen a man shot, he'd stiffened with fear and turned away from the slumped body, his heart hammering so hard he was afraid the guards would hear it.

Later that same day, when he watched a guard kick a man to the ground for walking too slowly, his fear turned to anger. Anger was better, but it was still dangerous. Looking down at the old man's bleeding body, limp as a sack of feed, Alexander took his fury and bottled it up with all the other dangerous thoughts that could get him killed.

I have to get tougher, he told himself. *No, not tougher, harder. Numb.* Being strong didn't help. Not when the guards had guns and whips. Any one of them could walk up to him, stick a gun to his head and pull the trigger. And there was nothing he could do about it; no way to stop them, no matter how strong he was. Alexander looked down at the ropy muscles along his arms. He'd been strong once. Almost as strong as his father who had legs like tree trunks. Alexander wiped the sweat from his forehead with the heel of his hand and wondered whether he'd recognize his father if he saw him. He looked down at his boots. They were his father's boots. After the Hungarian police had marched his father from their farm with his hands tied behind his back, Alexander had fled to the stable and found his father's old riding boots by the back door. He was only ten at the time and they'd been too big for him so he'd put them in a box and hidden them at the back of his cupboard. Four years later they were still two sizes too big, but they were the first thing he'd pulled on when the police stormed the farm a second time. He'd worn them ever since, keeping them by his head when he slept at night so they wouldn't be stolen. The worn leather carried his father's scent and the smell of the stables and it made him feel a little less alone.

"A10567."

"*Yavol.*" Alexander stepped forwards. He'd heard his number called dozens of times since coming to Birkenau, but he still felt the sting of it, every time. The guard with the clipboard who'd called his number didn't look up, just moved his pen further down the page.

The band tuned their instruments and, as the first of the labour units filed back into camp through the main gate, the conductor tapped his baton on his stand. The man had a faded cap on his head and a black space where a tooth had once been, but his eyes were still bright and his movements quick. Alexander had heard that the band members slept on beds with straw pallets and received extra rations. That they ate cheese with their bread and drank water when they were thirsty. Alexander could rope a cow from fifty metres and come to a sliding-stop on a horse from a flat-out gallop but he couldn't play the violin if his life depended on it. He stared at the conductor and tried not to hate him. I need to work, he thought. If I'm of use to the Nazis, I'll be fed.

The returning prisoners trudged through the gate in time to the music, their heads bent low, skin stretched over bone. The stronger ones carried the dead. They stacked the bodies like bits of rotten wood and fell into line to be counted. No one pitied those who had died. Alexander wondered if the men closest to the bodies saw them at all, or just saw through them, to the pockets they might empty or the boots they might steal. Maybe they were all numb. Maybe the only prisoners who continued to draw breath in Birkenau were those without a heart.

A German officer in a black uniform glanced onto a podium and shouted for sixty men to replace the quarry workers who'd died that day. No one volunteered. Quarry workers usually didn't last more than a week. The guards plucked the stronger looking inmates from the line and sent them to stand beside the men who worked the quarry. The officer in the black uniform glanced up from his notes and instructed his guards to collect a cook, two tailors and a bricklayer to replace the men in those units who had died. Hands flew up but Alexander's arm remained by his side. If he were older, if he were an accountant or a carpenter, if he knew how to cook or sew or weld, he could avoid the quarry and secure a place in a labour detail that worked indoors.

Alexander wanted to work. He was used to working. *Make yourself useful*, his father used to say, and Alexander would rush from the farmhouse to the stable to muck out the stalls or water the horses. Water. Alexander licked his lips. They were cracked and dry and tasted of blood. He needed water. He looked down at his grubby hands and dusty pants. Alexander hadn't showered in five weeks. Not since that first day in Birkenau. He shuddered, recalling the cool water that had dripped from the rusted pipes and the laughter of the naked men as they kissed each other's cheeks when the first drop fell. He hadn't understood their strange reaction – not until later that night in the barrack when he asked the block leader if he knew where the children from the trains had been sent.

"I have a sister." He choked on the last word as the Polish guard grabbed him by the collar and dragged him to the door.

"There are two types of shower blocks in Birkenau." The Pole grimaced. "The one you were sent to where you get wet and the other one" – he pointed at a grey brick building hidden behind a stand of fir trees – "where you don't."

"I don't understand," Alexander said, regretting the words as soon as he'd spoken them.

"Gas." The block leader spat the word at Alexander. "They use gas."

Alexander and the remaining men were marched back to their block. Another trainload of Hungarians had been squeezed into his barrack during roll-call and Alexander pushed past them to wait in line for his dinner. He hadn't eaten since midday and the watery soup he'd swallowed for lunch only intensified his hunger so that it tore at him. He heard a voice behind him ask "Where are you from?" but he didn't turn around.

"I'm from Medzev," the boy persisted. Alexander rolled his eyes. The new boys were all the same. They were looking for an ally, for someone to help them make sense of their surroundings. There was nothing he could say to make sense of this place. The SS wanted them dead. It didn't make sense, but they had guns, so it didn't have to.

Alexander stepped away from the boy, loosened his belt and unhooked his bowl. His hunger was vicious. When he reached the front of the line he held out his bowl and the block leader dropped a brick of grey bread and a sliver of sausage into it.

Alexander sat on the floor, cross-legged. The block leader handed out the last of the bread and turned to face the men sprawled on the ground.

"I'm your block leader." He addressed the new inmates. "They call me 'Bloody Mietek'."

Alexander had heard the speech dozens of times but it still felt like the block leader was directing the words at him.

"You'll find out why." Mietek spoke through his teeth. He was an ugly, small man with clay-coloured eyes and a crooked nose and Alexander wondered whether his sadistic streak had anything to do with his jagged left ear, which Alexander guessed had been torn away in a fight, leaving just a nub of flesh.

"There are only two things to remember in this barrack." Mietek smiled, revealing yellow teeth.

"One: do as I tell you. And two: don't try to escape. The only way out of here is through the chimney." The boy from Medzev looked confused and, for a moment, Alexander felt bad about how he'd treated him and wondered whether he should pull the boy aside later and talk to him: explain the showers that leaked gas and the smoke from the ovens. But then the boy would think that Alexander wanted to be his friend and Alexander didn't want friends. Not when there was every chance that tomorrow, when he woke up, they'd be gone.

Bloody Mietek threw down needles, thread and a bundle of cloth, and instructed the new men to take two triangles of coloured fabric and a rectangle of material with their number printed on it and sew the patches onto their jackets. The triangles were all yellow. Jews wore two yellow triangles, sewn together to form a Star of David, like the one Alexander had been forced to wear back home. There were other colours in the camp. Alexander had seen pink, black and violet triangles. The man Alexander had slept beside last week wore a red triangle on his shirt. He'd told Alexander to watch out for the green triangles. They were the professional criminals: the thieves, arsonists and murderers. Mietek wore a green triangle.

"Welcome to your new home." The block leader let the men take in their surroundings. The inmates looked at the three tier plank beds. There were no mattresses on the boards, just bits of straw that smelled like dung and thin, grey blankets. The walls were bare and the floor was grimy. A chimney flue ran the length of the barrack which was bookended by the block leader's room at one end and a row of containers smeared with excrement at the other.

"Enjoy your stay." He snatched a plank of wood from beside the door. "Now get outside." He swung at the nearest man and Alexander ran for the door. Men rushed to escape the block leader's reach, tripping over each other as they fled outside. Alexander reached the latrine hut, found an empty hole in the concrete slab, pulled down his pants and sat down on the bench. Even though it was summer, the floor was slimy with mud and the room was damp.

"*Scheissen!*" Mietek commanded, lowering his stick. It was hard to shit on command, sitting shoulder to shoulder with the next frightened man. Especially when your stomach was empty, but it would be hours before he would be allowed back to the latrines, so Alexander tried.

"You finished yet?" The man staring down at

Alexander reached out to nudge him. Alexander kicked out at the man and he moved down the line, rubbing his shin. There were only fifty-eight holes bored into the concrete bench, five minutes to do your business and hundreds of men. Fights broke out and the stronger men won. The man who'd nudged Alexander was tussling an older prisoner for an empty seat, three holes down. Alexander covered his ears and tried to block out the shouting and the sound of men straining to empty their bowels and, beyond the hut, the sound of dogs barking and guns firing. He craved quiet but there was nowhere in the camp where he could hide from the noise. There wasn't enough room or enough food, he thought, standing to wipe himself with a scrap of lining torn from his jacket. There were too many people, too many Nazis and dogs and guns, too much noise.

Back in Hungary, Alexander had avoided Košice's busy city streets, preferring the countryside's gaping spaces and endless sky. Part of him had been relieved when the order came that Jews weren't allowed to continue at school. He'd grown tired of the taunting and the banners decorated with swastikas which lined the streets. He hated the blaring loudspeakers strung from lampposts and the signs that read:

Jews not allowed. He loathed being trapped indoors, behind a desk, when all he wanted to do was ride his horse into the hills. And here I am, he thought, trapped behind barbed wire. He leaned over a rusted basin, washed the stains from his square of lining and walked back to the barrack.

Mietek turned the lights out and the men climbed onto their bunks. The boy next to Alexander closed his eyes and slept. Alexander didn't say goodnight. There was always someone in the barrack who didn't wake up the next day. So why say goodnight, he thought, when what you really mean is goodbye. Alexander turned away from the boy and stared at the wall. The wooden barrack had once been a horse stable and Alexander could still see the rings on the walls where the horses had been tethered. He'd slept in a stable before, the night his workhorse, Sari, had given birth to her foal, but the room had been warm and had smelled of leather and oats.

Alexander lay on the splintered wood, fighting sleep. He hadn't had a full night's sleep since the day he'd arrived in Birkenau. Every time he slipped into sleep, he saw his sister disappear into a grey brick building: the shower block where you didn't get wet. He wished he had a photograph of Lili, so he could look at his sister when he woke. A photo of her smiling face so he could banish her screams. Just one picture of the family so he could remember his mother's dark eyes, his father's crooked smile and his sister's blonde curls. There were nights he missed them so badly that the only thing he could do to stop himself crying out was to dig his nails into his palms. He unfurled a hand and traced the small crescent-shaped scars carved into his skin until his eyes grew heavy and sleep pulled him under.

"Steh auf!"

Alexander woke to the sharp sound of a whistle and Mietek's mean voice.

The block leader grabbed his plank of wood and Alexander leaped from his bunk. He didn't need to dress; he slept in his clothes. Breakfast was a cup of coffee. It tasted rank but it was hot and wet so Alexander drank it. The block leader threw out a handful of beet peels and ten men threw themselves on the scraps.

"Time for muster!" Mietek swung his plank at the nearest body. Alexander ran for the door and fell into line for the walk to the roll-call square. Another blue sky day, he thought, another day staring down the barrel of a gun and daring himself to hold its gaze.

"Don't let her know you're scared," his father had said to him the first time Alexander had sat on Sari's back. He was three. Sari was five: a gentle, hard-working mare with big kind eyes. Still, he'd been frightened when he'd felt the animal under him. It was one thing to climb onto the fence railing and pat the horse's brown mane, or sit in the milk cart beside his father and watch Sari's ears flick backwards and forwards as she trotted along. But another altogether to climb onto her broad back and feel her muscles shift under him.

Don't show the bastards you're scared.

Alexander stood in the baking heat and waited for the men to form their labour units. Caps on. Caps off. Men collapsing around him. Lunch was a bowl of gritty cabbage soup. Alexander tipped his bowl and licked it clean. He'd learned not to gulp down his meals. He drank slowly, paying attention to every sliver of cabbage, fixing his mind on the way the broth felt sliding down his parched throat. He'd been on his feet for six hours, had fifteen minutes for lunch, and here he was again, back under the mean sun, fighting his hunger and fear. He blotted the sweat from his face with his sleeve and counted down the hours until dinner.

When the labour units filed back into camp, the guard in the black uniform took the podium, cleared his throat and ran through the list of skilled workers needed to replace the day's dead. He called for three carpenters, a chemist, two mechanics and a metal worker. Men edged forwards and raised their hands. Alexander toed the dirt and waited for the whistle that marked the end of evening roll-call. His thirst was fierce and his stomach hurt. The block of bread he'd demolished the previous night lay in his stomach like a stone.

The guard tucked his clipboard under his arm and scanned the faces of the men assembled below him. "… horses."

Alexander lifted his head as he caught the end of the sentence. Three arms shot up in front of him. Had he heard right? After six weeks of roll-calls, waiting and watching, while other boys, smarter boys, more skilled boys, left his barrack for beds with clean sheets, had the guard spoken of horses?

Alexander looked up at the guard's face, at his lips, frozen into a grimace, and willed him to speak. To repeat what he'd said so Alexander could be sure. The man pointed to each of the men in turn, and waved them from the line.

"That's three of you. We need four men experienced with horses. Anyone else?"

Alexander's hand flew up just as the man beside him raised his arm. The guard turned to look at

Alexander and the prisoner beside him. He pointed a stubby finger and cleared his throat.

"You. Fourth from the end. We'll take you!"

Chapter 2

Alexander lowered his arm. He looked down at his hands and saw that they were trembling. The guard had chosen *him*. No more drills, no more standing under the hot sun for hours on end. Alexander's mind raced. He wasn't going to dig ditches or cart rocks. He'd be working with horses. He'd be sleeping in a new barrack and he'd be well fed. There'd be cheese and marmalade and soups thick with vegetables. And horses. He felt the corners of his mouth curl upward.

Stop it, he thought. A smile could get you killed. His smile fell away but the warm feeling stayed, so he tucked it away in a place deep down, a place the Nazis couldn't reach.

"Häftlinge folgt mir!" One of the guards turned on his heel and Alexander and the other men hurried after him. They didn't stop at their barrack to pack their belongings. The men wore everything they owned: a pair of striped pyjamas and a cap, a rusted

bowl looped onto a belt and a pair of camp clogs or their own worn-out shoes. Alexander marched past the colourless barracks and the smoking chimneys, taking a deep breath when he stepped beyond the main gate. It felt good to breathe clean air and move his arms and legs. He looked into the darkness at the pitted dirt road that snaked away from the camp and wondered where they were headed. The boy in front of him glanced back at him, a smile crinkling the skin around his eyes but Alexander didn't smile back. He didn't pay the boy any attention, not until he saw him swoop on the guard's discarded cigarette butt and slip it into his pocket.

The guard stopped at a fence and raised his gun. He motioned the prisoners through a gate, above which a sign read *Arbeit Macht Frei* – Work Brings Freedom. Alexander's stomach tightened. This wasn't what he'd expected. The place looked just like Birkenau: steel, barbed wire and rows of blinding floodlights.

"*Halt!*" The guard raised his hand and stopped outside a double-storey brick building where an inmate wearing a green triangle waited at the door. He carried a leather belt in his hand and peered down at the men, his dark eyes slits above his pointed nose.

"These the new men for the Horse Platoon?" he enquired of the guard.

The guard slid a cigarette between his lips and nodded.

Platoon? Alexander bristled. Who did they think they were fooling? Alexander knew he was lucky to be looking after the Nazis' horses but it was still slave labour. They weren't a platoon. You don't murder the families of your platoon officers! Alexander glared at the inmate.

"Welcome to Auschwitz. I'm your new block leader." The man with the green triangle introduced himself. "I run this barrack. Your *kapo*, who will come for you tomorrow, is in charge of your platoon. He'll take you to the stables. The Commander of the Horse Platoon, Herr Ziegler, will meet you there." Block leader, kapo, Nazi – all ugly words, Alexander thought, words that cost him the farm and his family.

The block leader kicked the door open and Alexander saw a set of stairs and beyond it, a row of three tier bunks. Bunks with straw mattresses, smooth, white sheets and blankets. The beds were big; the beds were huge. Alexander's eyes grew round. It was like a palace compared to the last barrack.

"Inside. *Schnell!*" The block leader waited for the prisoners to enter the barrack, before following them in. The guard stood in the doorway, his hand on his gun.

"Let's take a look at you. Line up." The block leader surveyed the men with cold eyes. Alexander puffed out his chest and pinched his cheeks to redden them.

The block leader stopped in front of each of the men in turn, and asked them to touch their toes or stick out their tongue. He seemed to wear a permanent sneer, and Alexander noticed his lips didn't close all the way, exposing his crooked teeth. Alexander waited his turn. The block leader looked him up and down as if he was a cow at a farm sale.

"Take them to the showers," the block leader spat.

The showers? Alexander began to panic. The guard raised his gun and the men hurried out the door after him.

"What about the horses?" Alexander croaked, but the guard didn't answer.

"Doesn't he want us?" Alexander tapped the shoulder of the man in front of him. "What did we do wrong?" Alexander knew about the showers. He knew that the heads leaked gas, not water. "Why can't he just send us back to Birkenau?" Alexander raised his voice, "I'll go back to Birkenau."

The man in front of him turned back and glared. "I'm not going back to Birkenau. And neither are you."

"*Ruhe!*" the guard snapped and Alexander fell silent.

He stepped into the brick building, left his dusty clothes on the bench and fell into line, lifting his eyes to the dirty grey ceiling and the shower heads spaced a metre apart. "I'm coming, Lili," he whispered, as the heavy wooden door slammed shut behind him. "You can stop crying now. I'll be with you soon."

And then the water pelted down.

A prisoner with a green triangle grabbed Alexander and scraped a blunt razor over his head. A toothless German clipped his body hair and mopped a dripping rag over his skin. It smelled like the spray his mother used to clean the kitchen, caustic and bitter. He walked back to the barrack, dripping, his scalp stinging where it had been nicked, his skin burning.

"That's better." The block leader spat out a number and a man stepped forwards for inspection. Alexander looked down at the tattoo on his arm and thought of the cows corralled at the farm, waiting to be branded. His father had shown him how to use the branding iron when he was nine and Alexander had spent the summer burning numbers onto the backsides of cows. The animals hadn't submitted quietly, Alexander remembered. They'd squealed and spurted shit over his boots.

Alexander hated the tattoo. But he was proud of the jagged scar on his left knee. It reminded him of the time he'd clipped a fence as he sailed over it on the back of a horse. The puckered skin on his right shoulder was a parting gift from a bucking bull. He'd received many bruises and bumps at the hands of an animal and he wore them with pride.

But not the tattoo. Or the Star of David he'd been forced to wear when the Germans took over Hungary. The yellow star with the word *Jude* stamped on it had marked him a Jew and that meant he could be ignored by teachers, refused entry at the cinema, chased from the soccer field and spat on in the street. The star meant he was different. Alexander didn't keep kosher or walk to synagogue on Saturdays. He didn't pray to God or understand Hebrew. He didn't feel any different from the boys at school or the other farmers' sons.

He looked from the men standing beside him in soiled, ragged clothes to the guard, dressed in a uniform, a cigarette dangling from his lips. His pants were tucked into shiny, black boots and his brass-buttoned coat was cinched at the waist by a gleaming silver belt. Alexander narrowed his eyes and read the words embossed on the buckle: *Gott mit uns* – God is with us. If God was with the Nazis, Alexander thought, then who was looking out for the Jews?

"A10567." Alexander was the last to be called. He stepped forwards.

"You'll do," the block leader said, his lips pursed in a cynical smile. "You might even live to see the New Year," he paused, "if you do as I say." Alexander swallowed hard.

"You'll join the Horse Platoon tomorrow. You four will replace the four men who were shot today." The block leader waited so the words could sink in. "They were shot because the horses they were responsible for ate poison brambles." The block leader laughed, a thin acidic laugh. "Don't worry," he said, "the horses are fine now."

Alexander clenched his fists. *Just get through the day*, he breathed. *Get through today.*

A whistle sounded and a column of men approached the open door of the barrack. The guard stepped aside to let them pass. Alexander watched them file into the room and either drag themselves up the stairs or collapse onto a bunk, their faces glazed with sweat. He guessed there were around two hundred of them split between two floors and learned from eavesdropping on their conversations that they were tailors, machinists, doctors and welders. All of them worked in special units like the Corpse Squad, whose job it was to collect the dead, or the Clerical Detail, who attended to the camp books. They had insect legs and shaved heads like the walking dead he'd left behind in Birkenau, but hope flickered in their red-rimmed eyes. Alexander could see that although they were worn-out and hungry, they hadn't lost the will to live.

The block leader pointed to four bunks. "They're yours," he said to the new inmates, "and take these." He handed each of the men a clean cup. Alexander looped it onto his belt next to his rusted bowl and took the bunk on the middle tier, three from the end. A prisoner wearing faded pants and a crumpled coat with a purple triangle stitched onto the left breast lay on the bunk below his. His face was gaunt − a skeleton's face − and dangling from his veined hand was a silver cross. Alexander had heard that the clergy wore purple triangles but this was the first purple triangle he'd seen.

Another whistle sounded and the men who had filed into the barrack began to undress. Alexander peeled off his shirt and pulled off his boots and, tucking them under his arm, followed the men through a door to a bathroom, his eyes widening as he entered the room and saw, along one wall, a row of shower heads and along another, a bank of toilets. With seats.

He stuffed his bundle of clothes under a bench and stepped under a shower to relieve his stinging skin, tilting his head up to catch the murky water in his mouth. He found some soap on the floor to wash the acid smell from his body, but no matter how hard he scrubbed he couldn't wash away the memory of his sister stepping from the cattle car.

He turned off the tap. Two men were leaning over a rusted basin, peering into the cracked glass that hung from the wall.

"You've got to shave every day." One of the men scraped a switchblade across his stubbled cheek and turned to his friend. "Get your hands on a piece of glass before the next selection." He splashed water onto his face. "Your scraped cheeks will have colour and you'll look younger." Alexander shuddered. He didn't want to hop up and down on the spot or do star jumps to prove his fitness for work. He'd hoped he'd seen the last of the selections now that he was part of a special unit.

He pulled on his clothes and waited for supper, wondering if, like Bloody Mietek, the block leader would toss them scraps of food to fight over. He'd overheard the men talking about the block leader. They referred to him as the Rat, on account of his face, and Alexander thought it a fitting nickname. He scanned the room for someone lugging a soup tureen but instead saw men, clustered in groups, talking. Some sat on the floor, others lay on bunks. A few men huddled by the open door, smoking. The boy who'd snatched the guard's cigarette stub stood in a corner, talking to a group of men.

Alexander watched as the boy shook each of the men's hands in turn, reaching into his pocket before the last man took his hand. Alexander craned his head and saw the boy pull the cigarette stub from his pocket and hand it to the man, before he took something in return, something withered and green. The stem of a pear, or a potato peel, maybe. Alexander rubbed his stomach and tried to soothe his hunger. The men next to him were trading chicken soup recipes and Alexander wanted to cry because, though the men filled their free hours talking about food, what they really meant was that they missed home. If they discussed barley soup and beans instead of their wives and daughters, if they focused on crumbed fish instead of their dead relatives, maybe they could pretend none of this was happening.

The cigarette stub boy crossed the room and stopped in front of Alexander. "We get bread for dinner – same as Birkenau – but cheese is a definite possibility." The boy took his hands from his pockets and Alexander saw that he was holding an apple core.

"Want to split it?" The boy spoke quickly.

"What do you want in return?" Alexander narrowed his eyes. No one gave food away, not unless they wanted something in return.

"The name's Isidor Finkler, but my friend's call me Isi." The boy extended his right hand.

Alexander didn't shake it. He sighed. The boy wanted to be his friend. "No thanks," he said. If he took the food, sooner or later the boy would ask a favour of him. He'd want Alexander to look after him when he was ill or cover for him when he snuck from the barrack. He'd expect Alexander to give him food and Alexander would have to do it. *If* they were friends.

"Suit yourself," the boy said, biting into the apple and looking Alexander up and down. "How did you get into the men's camp, anyway? You don't look old enough."

The SS doctor who'd stood on the arrival platform

looking down at Alexander from the podium on his first day at Birkenau had said the same thing. Every time he saw Dr Mengele at a selection or a roll-call, Alexander was reminded of that horrible day, and now this freckled-face boy, with all his questions, had forced Alexander back there again, back to the very first selection.

It had been a Friday night. Alexander, Lili and their mother had been travelling for three days in the cramped cattle train. They weren't fed or given water and, after the first day, Alexander's mother had no food left in her bag to give them. Alexander had sat in the dark, knees drawn up to his face, watching the train tracks through the cracks in the floorboards. When he heard the cattle cars rumbling to a stop, he'd hoisted Lili onto his shoulders to peer through the small window above their heads.

"It's awful," she'd said. "There's nothing but barbed wire and rows of ugly sheds."

When the doors were flung open and Alexander jumped down, lifting his sister out after him, he saw that the place was worse than she'd described – much worse. They were told to line up in two columns: men and older boys in one column; women and children in the other. Alexander was fourteen. He stood next to his mother and took his sister's hand.

SS officers pulled men from their wives and sons from their fathers.

"Go with the men," his mother whispered, but Alexander shook his head. He'd promised his father he'd take care of them.

"Listen to your mother. Go with the men." A man in a striped jacket and drawstring pants grabbed Alexander's sleeve and shoved him towards the men. "Tell them you're sixteen."

Alexander shuffled forwards as the doctor stood on the podium in front of the men, pointing his baton to his left or right as each prisoner stopped before him.

"Alex!" A familiar voice. "It's me, Mendel." Alexander swung around to see his father's friend standing behind him.

"Mendel!" Alexander began, but the farmer cut him off.

"Alex, listen to me. The SS are pulling boys from the men's group before they get to the front of the line. Stand on my feet until we're near the podium – you'll look taller." Alexander frowned. "It's OK." Mendel dragged his crooked left foot forwards and showed Alexander his heavy boot. "It won't hurt."

The line drifted along.

Mendel took Alexander's hand and drew the boy

close. "Your father was a good friend to me. After I got polio and stopped working he still delivered the milk to our house, every day. Never charged us a *pengo*. Let me do this for you ... for him." Alexander took Mendel's hand and steadied himself on the man's feet.

"You go first," Mendel whispered, nudging Alexander ahead as they neared the podium.

"How old are you?" the doctor asked Alexander when it was his turn to be inspected. Mendel stood next to him, breathing heavily.

"Sixteen," Alexander said, remembering to lie.

The doctor took a step forwards. "Sixteen?" He looked Alexander in the eye and all Alexander could think to do was run. He turned from the podium and without a backwards glance, ran past an open-mouthed Dr Mengele, his guards and their dogs, and he didn't stop running, not until he was on the other side of the fence, buried in the crush of men selected to survive.

He'd waited for Mendel. Watched other men, at least ten men, file through the gate to join his group. He counted to one hundred and when his father's friend still hadn't come, he fought his way to the front of the group, and peering through the barbed wire, saw Mendel, limping to the left, dragging his crooked leg after him.

"How old am I?" Alexander shucked off the memories and looked into Isidor Finkler's green eyes. "Old enough."

Alexander was rich that night. The proud owner of half a loaf of bread and a stick of cheese. He meant to save some for the next day but he tore at the bread and devoured the cheese and, before he knew it, there was nothing left but the few crumbs that had fallen into his lap. He swept up the scraps and ate them too.

"So, where are you from?" Isidor swallowed the last of his bread and turned to Alexander. He would have answered the question — if only to shut the boy up — but Alexander didn't know what to say. Where *was* he from? He couldn't say Czechoslovakia, because when he was eight years old, his country was taken over by Hungary, and he couldn't say Hungary, because four years later the Germans occupied Hungary and forced them out. He couldn't even say the farm at 6 Gregor Lane, not after his family had been ordered to sign it over to one of his Aryan neighbours. He'd lost the house, the stables, his father's cattle and the horses.

"I'm from Debrecen," Isidor said, though Alexander

hadn't asked. "But I'm not going back. My father's dead."

Alexander looked away.

"Shot in the back of the head because he wouldn't hand over the keys to our apartment."

Alexander shook his head, then realized Isidor might misconstrue the gesture as sympathy. *I don't want to know your story,* he thought. *I've heard a hundred others just like it and I don't care.* Alexander wished he could say the words out loud, wished he was tough enough, mean enough, to tell the boy to shut up.

"My mother died in the ghetto," Isidor continued, but Alexander cut him off.

"Talking about it doesn't help," he said, staring into the boy's eyes. "Tomorrow is all that matters. Getting through the day and waking up tomorrow."

The Rat turned out the lights and Alexander climbed onto his bunk, lifted the tip of his spoon to the bedhead and carved the number forty-three into the wood. Forty-three days since he'd stepped from the cattle train and walked through the gates of Birkenau. Forty-three days and counting.

"Tomorrow," Isidor whispered, climbing up after Alexander and sinking into the straw mattress beside him. "Tomorrow will be a good day. Tomorrow we'll ride horses."

And despite himself, Alexander smiled. He thought of the long, dusty days ahead of him, the horses pressed close around him: brown-eyed chestnuts, blacks and roans. He'd rub them down, attend to their sores, feed them and groom them. On warm days he'd lead them out to graze and in winter, as the grass lost its flavour, he'd feed them hay and make warm straw beds for them. He wasn't sure whether the Horse Platoon were allowed to ride the horses into the woods, but even if he were ordered to run circles around a paddock strung with barbed wire, he'd be happy.

Tomorrow he'd ride horses.

Chapter 3

"*Alles raus!*"

Alexander opened his eyes and saw the Rat swing a hammer at a dented hubcap propped against the front door. The metallic clanging dragged the men from their dreams and one by one they opened their eyes and lifted their heads from their mattresses. Alexander swung his legs over the side of his bunk.

"*Aufstehen! Schnell! Schnell!*" The Rat dropped the hammer and started pulling men from their beds. Alexander yanked on his boots and leaped from his bunk. It was still dark, the night sky crammed with stars. He made his bed and darted across the hard concrete floor to the toilets.

By the time Alexander returned, his bunkmates were queuing for breakfast. He slipped into line and waited. His body craved food and Alexander hoped that the barrel the Rat had dragged into the centre of the room contained soup: a hot chicken broth or a hearty bean soup. The Rat pried the lid from the metal tureen and the smell of wormwood wafted into the room. It was coffee – the same dark, dirty water that they served in Birkenau. Alexander neared the front of the queue, his hunger woken by the loaf of bread he'd devoured at dinner, so that it ripped at his insides. He saw the boy in front of him lift his tin bowl to catch the liquid dripping off the Rat's ladle, heard the tinny clunk of metal hitting metal as the boy, impatient for food, stepped too close. The room grew quiet and the inmate, sensing his mistake, pulled his bowl from the Rat's spoon.

The block leader's rodent face grew more pointed. "You want coffee so bad?" he shouted. "So, drink." He thrust the boy's head into the tureen and held him there, face down in the murky water, for five long seconds, then ten. After fifteen seconds the boy's arms stopped flailing. Twenty seconds and the bubbles stopped. The Rat pulled the boy from the tureen and threw him to the floor where he lay, dripping and spluttering, but alive.

Alexander inched forwards and held out his bowl.

He noticed the priest's eyes follow him back to his bunk. Alexander lifted his bowl to his lips and drank the dirty water down. Every last drop. The priest stared up at him. He was still in bed.

"They're not going to bring you food," Alexander said. "And neither will I."

"Father Jablonski isn't hungry." The block leader grabbed Alexander's collar and pushed him towards the door. "*Geh Raus!* Outside! It's time for muster."

Alexander guessed it was around four am. The sky was black and the moon was close to the horizon. If he was back home, he'd be sneaking from the house to saddle his horse before dawn.

"Rows of five!" The Rat stopped under a flood-light, his pointed nose elongated under the lamp's glow.

Alexander fell into line and Isidor stood to attention beside him. "He's refusing to eat," Isidor whispered.

"Who?" Alexander whispered back.

"Father Jablonski." Isidor stared straight ahead and spoke through his teeth. "He's a Czech priest, imprisoned for speaking out against Hitler. After he saw a boy shot in the head at roll-call, he stopped eating."

A whistle sounded and the men were divided into their work details.

"Your kapo will take it from here. Do as he says." The block leader nodded at the man beside him. Alexander was surprised to find the kapo in the same striped uniform he wore. He looked him up and down. The kapo was a giant, almost two metres tall, Alexander guessed, though it was hard to tell as the man was stooped. Alexander watched him chew on a fingernail before spitting it out. He wore a yellow star on his blue-and-white shirt and grey trousers that were too short for his long, hairy legs. The pale sun crept over the horizon and Alexander saw that the man's skin was rough as leather, his nails chewed down to the quick.

The man dragged his feet as he walked between them, counting out aloud.

"Dwadzie cia osiem." He spat the words out in Polish. Twenty-eight. There were twenty-eight men in the Horse Platoon, twenty-nine including the kapo.

"Alles Raus!" he shouted into the nearest man's ear. The inmate stumbled, clasping his ear. A bemused SS officer looked on. The kapo swatted the inmate's hand away with a metal stick. *"Alles Raus!"* he screamed again, and the men hurried forwards.

The camp band struck up a march and Alexander walked through the open gate, Isidor behind him. Three girls with long, glossy hair and painted lips leaned out of a second floor window to watch the parade. Alexander stared up at the window, surprised to find women in the camp. He craned his neck to look past the women, hoping perhaps to catch a glimpse of his mother in the room behind them.

"You can't afford them, Jew-boy." An officer hurled a stone at Alexander's head and laughed. Alexander rubbed his ear where the stone had clipped him and looked up at the women again. They wore low-cut blouses and blew kisses to the officers.

"Whores," the man in front of Alexander swore under his breath.

Alexander kept walking. Up ahead the crematoria spewed dirty smoke into the sky. A black sadness settled over him. He thought he should say a prayer for his sister, but he didn't know the right words — the Hebrew words.

The sun rose in the sky and Alexander watched his shadow slip in front of him. He saw his bony arms swinging by his sides and his legs, like toothpicks, march in time to the music. He saw the silhouettes of the armed guards and their German shepherds straining at their leads and the dim outline of the birch trees that lined the entrance to the camp. When the inmates reached the main gate, the kapo shouted *"Mutzen ab!"* and the men pulled their caps from their heads and turned to face the right. Alexander copied them and turned to see an

SS officer watching as they passed, a high-ranking officer with a dozen badges pinned to his coat. He had dark bushy eyebrows and cold green eyes. The men walked past the checkpoint, put their caps back on and turned in unison to face the front. Alexander was a beat behind them. He swung his head around and hoped no one noticed.

Outside the camp, sparrows darted between the trees. Alexander watched them swoop between the branches and envied their freedom. He looked at the fields and the trees and the grass and the leaves, so green and so alive. His sister was dead but the sun was still shining.

"You'll be working for Herr Ziegler, Commander of the Horse Platoon." The kapo left the front of the column to march beside Alexander and Isidor. "He'll assign you a horse. The commander and the other officers pick up their horses most mornings. You'll work five am till midday, then one till six pm, seven days a week. Every morning you'll brush, feed and water your horse. You'll do the same at night. In between you'll clean the stable and prepare your horse's feed. Don't let the animal lose weight or condition."

Alexander could feel the kapo's eyes boring into him, but he didn't dare look up. "If I tell you that your officer requires his mount, saddle up his horse and be waiting outside for him when he arrives. Take your cap off and hold the stirrups for him. Once he's comfortable on the horse, hand him the reins and move away fast or he'll run you over." Alexander turned to look at the kapo, to see if his words were meant as a warning or a taunt, but the man had moved back up the line, his long legs carrying him to the front of the column.

Alexander wasn't worried. He knew how to handle horses. And working seven days a week didn't bother him. He was happy to escape Auschwitz for the stables. Back at home – before he was forced from the farm and taken to Birkenau – whenever he felt sad or confused he'd escape to the barn. If he couldn't sleep at night, he'd slip out the back door and creep from the house with a carrot or an apple. Just opening the stable door and stepping into the warm barn made him feel better. He loved the sweet smell of hay and the crunch of it under his boots. And the horses. He loved all of them: the plough horse, the mare who pulled the milk cart, the spirited Arabian his father bought to help herd the cattle, and the copper-coloured pony his parents gave Lili on her fifth birthday. But there was one he loved more than the rest. Sari. His father had bought the horse as a yearling and Alexander and the filly had grown up together. They'd both started out timid and knock-kneed but had become strong. Whenever he wasn't at school or doing chores, he'd lead her to the tall grass by the river or ride her out over the fields. He'd taught her to jump poles and fences and to come at his whistle. She came, not out of obedience, but because she wanted to be near him.

"So, is this horse thing difficult?" Isidor interrupted his thoughts. Alexander swung around to look at him. "I mean, I've been to a farm" – Isidor quickened his pace, his breath warm on Alexander's neck – "on a school trip. I milked a cow. How hard can it be?"

Alexander snapped his head forwards and clenched his fists. They were bookended by guards; the boy's mouth would get them both killed.

"I just need a few pointers," Isidor whispered.

Alexander swung his arms harder. When the men entered a forest, the kapo held up his giant hand and the inmates stopped. The officers slung their guns over their shoulders and sat down in the tall grass to smoke while the prisoners stood in a cluster and waited.

"Were you serious?" Alexander asked Isidor when he saw the other inmates talk among themselves.

"You've never worked with horses?"

Isidor shrugged. "I'm a city boy."

Alexander stared at him. He needn't have worried about the boy becoming his friend. They had nothing in common. Isidor lived in the city and Alexander hated the city. He hated the stinking smoke and the ugly factories. He hated the overcrowded streets and the tiny apartments with their concrete backyards. Alexander lived to ride horses. Isidor had never sat on one. Alexander deserved this job. Isidor had stolen it from some poor farmer whose hand hadn't shot up fast enough at roll-call.

"So, I figured you can teach me," Isidor said.

"And what do I get out of it?" Alexander shot back.

"My friendship," Isidor ventured.

Friendship? Alexander almost laughed out loud. A friend was someone you played stickball with. Someone you clambered up trees after and waded into rivers with to catch frogs. A friend was someone you spent your winters with building snow forts. A boy like Anton Hudak. If Anton was still his friend.

"I'm not looking for a friend," Alexander said, wondering if he'd ever be able to erase the image of his best friend standing at the bus stop in Hlavna

Street wearing a brown uniform and a swastika armband.

"We all need friends," Isidor whispered, "especially here."

"You're wrong." If he'd learned anything these past few months it was that to care meant to be weak. His survival depended on him being impervious to other people's feelings, as well as his own. If I was soft, he thought, would I have been able to throw a baby over a fence? Alexander's fingernails punctured his palms as he recalled his aunt and uncle returning from Budapest to find the rest of their family behind the ghetto walls. Ruth and Jacob had left for Budapest, and had asked Alexander's mother to mind their baby while they were gone. A week later the Altmanns were forced from their farm. With no one to leave her sister's four-month-old baby with, Alexander's mother had taken Sammy into the ghetto with them. *Throw him over*, his aunt Ruth had whispered, reaching her fingers through the gaps in the fence to stroke Sammy's face. *Quick, before the guards come.* Alexander hadn't wanted to, but he'd had no choice. *You're a rock*, he'd told himself. *You're a brick wall.* Do it. He lifted his cousin above his head and, with trembling hands, launched Sammy into the air.

Alexander's heart skipped a beat, as it had that day in the ghetto when his aunt, reaching up with splayed fingertips, caught the child.

"I can help you," Isidor continued. "I know people and I know how this place works. I know where to get food and I know where to find socks."

Alexander wriggled his blistered toes. If he didn't help the boy, Isidor would end up endangering a horse because of his inexperience and it might end badly for all of them. Really badly. He had no choice. Alexander rubbed his stomach and wondered what to ask for first – a carrot or an apple.

Alexander spoke quickly as the guards rose to their feet. "The first tip is never walk behind a horse or directly in front of it. They're both blind spots and the horse will run over the top of you or swing into you and knock you flat." Isidor's eyes widened and Alexander sneered. Not so cocky now, are you, city boy?

Alexander heard the horses before he saw them. The hills echoed with the sound of their pounding hooves and, as he neared the gate, the air grew thick with the unmistakable smell of saddle leather. He walked through the gate and breathed in, saw the acres of green and the glossy manes. So many horses.

The inmates filed into the yard and the horses

stopped, their ears pricked. A dozen of them walked to the paddock fence and, as Alexander walked past, a soft-eyed chestnut put her face forwards. Alexander reached out to stroke her neck. Horses didn't care if you were a Jew or a German. He ran his hands over her soft skin. As long as you fed them. As long as you were fair.

Chapter 4

"*Vorrücken!*" the kapo yelled, brandishing his stick. Alexander pulled his hand from the mare and hurried through the yard. Squinting into the sun, he saw that the paddock was the size of three soccer fields, and beyond it was more green – acres of pasture on which the horses could graze.

Potatoes! Alexander's heart drummed against his chest. Just beyond the fenced pasture was a rectangle of tilled ground streaked with flowering shrubs in neat rows: a potato field. Alexander's mouth watered. Mashed potatoes. His stomach twisted. Fried potatoes, potatoes drenched in sour cream...

"*Halt! Stillen!*" the kapo yelled and the men stopped next to a small fenced enclosure. Beside the ring was a stable, above the entrance a painted sign which read: *On the back of a horse is paradise on earth.* Alexander stared up at the building. It was nothing like the stable his father had built for their five horses, their goat and his dog, Spitz, but the sight of its slanted tin roof and wide stable doors catapulted Alexander back home to the farm at 6 Gregor Lane and the garden tucked behind the stable, sewn with corn, potato and beans. Who are you kidding? he thought. The farm was nothing like that by the time you left. The Germans had taken most of the horses, trampled the vegetable patch and dismantled the tractor for spare parts.

This stable was much larger, big enough to hold thirty horses.

"*Achtung!*" the kapo yelled and the men stood to attention. A dozen guards stood facing the men, their hands on their guns. The kapo stiffened and looked to the gate. Alexander followed his gaze and, through a cloud of dust, saw first a galloping horse – its white coat gleaming in the sun, its mane slapping its neck – and then its rider. They pounded towards the inmates in huge strides that tore the grass under the horse's thundering hooves, and came to a stop centimetres from where the men stood. To ride again – Alexander's breath caught in his throat – to feel the reins biting into your hands and that powerful engine beneath you. Alexander wanted to run his hands over the stallion's strong flanks. It was an Arabian, deep chested and strong in the quarters, about four years old and fifteen hands high.

"The Commander of the Horse Platoon!" the kapo announced, straightening his shoulders. "Commander Ziegler." Alexander looked up at the officer sitting elegantly on his horse, the creases in his uniform razor sharp, his jodhpurs tucked into black riding boots. He had a gun at his side and a whip in his hand. His iron legs gripped the horse, but he didn't reach down to pat the animal. He slid off the horse and dropped the reins. The kapo shoved one of the new boys to pick the straps up off the ground.

Alexander looked up into the commander's face. His eyes were the colour of grey slate, his nose small and straight, his jaw hard. Alexander had watched officers like the commander ride their steeds past his farm. When he was eight, the Hungarian military marched past on their way to the city, to claim it from the Czechs. He remembered his sister's fascination with the Hungarian uniforms, how she'd admired the curved cockerel feathers pinned to the officers' tall, pointed hats. Alexander hadn't cared that the Hungarians were taking Košice; he'd been mesmerised by the cavalry as they galloped by. Six years later, when the German army occupied the country, Alexander barely registered their horses. All he saw were the columns of foot soldiers passing in front of his gate and the tanks and canons barrelling after them.

By then, Alexander knew that the SS were tearing through Europe, burning down synagogues and looting shops. They'd emptied whole cities of Jews, sending them away by train or forcing them into ghettos. His mother had begged him to escape before the Hungarian police came to take him, but he'd refused. With his father gone he was the man of the house. His mother and Lili needed him. He wouldn't desert them – or the horses.

The commander's horse had imperious grey eyes like its master. It was a purebred and Alexander would have bet the commander had chosen him for his fine breeding, refined head and arched neck. He would have checked that the horse's feet were sound and his bones strong. He would have been pleased by the stallion's perfect white coat.

The Arabian stamped its feet and shook its mane, demanding attention.

"Take Serafin inside and strip his tack," the commander ordered the boy who had taken the reins. He turned to face the inmates. "I want all the horses rubbed down, fed and watered. Now get moving." He cracked his whip against the side of his boot. The snapping sound made Alexander jump. He'd handled lots of riding crops, but none as long or mean as the commander's. The whip had a wooden handle and a single thick black leather strap, and Alexander wondered whether the commander used it to tame animals or men.

The stablehands collected their horses from the paddock and followed the commander into the stable, leaving Alexander, Isidor and the other new stablehand standing outside.

"Mach Schnell!" the kapo yelled, pointing at the stable. "Don't keep the commander waiting."

Alexander hurried into the barn.

"You!" The commander pointed to the man on Alexander's right. "Take that horse. The black filly." He pointed to a stall. "And you." He brought his whip down next to Isidor's feet, sending dust flurrying around the boy's ankles. "You get the last horse, the Hungarian thoroughbred over there."

"How old are you?" The commander took a step towards Alexander.

"Sixteen," Alexander said. It was a lie, but a lie that would keep him alive and besides, he felt older than fourteen. Much older. The war – and this place – had aged him.

"Follow me." The commander led Alexander to the stall next to Isidor's. "You claim you have experience with horses, tell me about this one." The commander slid the bolt from the stall door and swung it open to reveal a miniature pony. It looked just like Lili's pony, Strudel, a Hucul with a reddish brown coat.

"It's a pony," Alexander began, and the commander folded his arms against his chest and waited. "A Hucul. They're hardy animals, used to working in rugged terrain, but they're gentle so they're good with children." He wondered if the animal had a name. He scratched the pony behind her ears and smoothed its nose. He had only one chance to make a good impression.

"I'm not interested in the breed. Tell me about this particular pony." The commander stepped back and invited Alexander to examine the animal.

"Well…" Alexander began, not sure what the commander wanted to hear. "She's a chestnut so she has black skin under her coppery coat." The commander nodded. "She's about thirteen-hands high and her feet look sound. Strong hooves," Alexander continued, lifting each of the pony's legs, before opening her mouth to examine her teeth. "I'd guess she's three years old." The commander remained silent. "Her ribs are well sprung." Alexander ran his hand over the pony's coat and tried to still his shaking hands. Horses sensed if you were tense and it made them anxious.

"Let's see if you know what to do with her." The commander's smile was ugly. He pointed to a row of shelves on the back wall and Alexander hurried from the stall to collect a currycomb and a thick-bristled brush. He found them crammed between a gleaming leather saddle and a bridle. The stable was well equipped. There were halters, lead lines, hoof picks, blankets, buckets for water and a metal trough for feed. There was protective cream for the pink skin around the horses' noses and fly-fringes to keep the insects away. Alexander thought of all the things he'd left behind on the farm and the things he'd packed for the train but had to leave on the platform: his calfskin gloves – a present from his father – a black-and-white photo of Sari and the miniature wooden horse his grandfather had carved out of oak. He grabbed a hoof pick and ran back to the stall.

He started with the currycomb, moving in broad circles over the pony's back and hindquarters, soothing her with his voice until she relaxed under his touch. He skirted the sensitive skin on her legs and picked her feet out with the hoof pick, checking her shoes for damage. By the time he was finished his shirt was plastered to his back and his arms were streaked with dirt, but the pony looked beautiful. Alexander breathed in her horsey smell. It was wrong to say he was happy, but he found himself smiling.

"Tack her up," the commander ordered, cracking his whip against his boot. "Heinz, show the boy where Chestnut's tack is kept."

Chestnut, Alexander thought. *The pony has a name, not a number.*

The kapo swung the door open and the commander left the stall.

"Her saddle is over there." The kapo raised his giant hand and pointed to a saddle hanging from a peg on the back wall. It had a small seat with a leather horn – the type of saddle children used when they weren't accustomed to riding. Alexander grabbed the saddle.

"Sure you can handle a horse that size?" Isidor walked up and grabbed a saddle blanket. "I'm in the stall next door to you, so if you need any help..." A smile split his face.

"She's a pony, not a horse." Alexander rolled his eyes.

"Either way, *you* should've got the commander's horse," Isidor whispered. "Do you reckon the commander knew he was giving his horse to a Nussbaum?"

"A Nussbaum?" Alexander shook his head, confused.

"The boy who got the commander's horse."

Alexander waited.

"I went to school with him. His father, Isak Nussbaum, is a breeder. *Was* a breeder," Isidor corrected himself. "The boy's family owned the biggest stud farm in Poland. That big white horse…"

"Stallion," Alexander butted in. "A male horse is a stallion, unless he's been castrated, then he's a gelding."

Isidor nodded.

"The commander's stallion," he said, "probably came from Nussbaum's farm."

Alexander grabbed a lead line and returned to his stall. There were guards in the stable, but if he crouched down behind the stall door, they couldn't see him. He bent over the pony and breathed in her dusty smell. The last time he'd been this close to a horse, he'd been saying goodbye to Sari. He'd fallen asleep in the stall and woken at midnight to find his horse lying on her side with her neck pressed against his back. He hoped their neighbour, who now owned their farm, was looking after her. He hoped Radomir Hudak was feeding her twice a day and washing the mud from her hocks.

"Are you done?" The kapo swung the door open and Alexander jerked away from the pony, reminding himself that the animal was a means to survival, not a pet. *No getting soft*, he said to himself. *Soft is dangerous.* He swung the saddle blanket onto the pony, smoothed out the wrinkles and slid the saddle onto it.

"Bring her out," the kapo ordered. Alexander slipped a halter over the pony's nose and led Chestnut from the stall.

"The children like to ride her." The kapo lowered his voice. "It's a distraction from the gloominess."

Children? Something stirred in the pit of Alexander's belly. What children? He dragged on the rope and hurried to the stable door. His legs felt rubbery. He knew it couldn't be Lili — wouldn't be Lili — but still the thought galloped towards him.

"Make sure they wear a helmet," the kapo called after him. "It's only once around the ring, then it's the next child's turn."

Alexander took a deep breath and stepped into the yard.

Chapter 5

Alexander's shoulders slumped when he saw the children waiting in a neat line outside the enclosure. The girls wore pinafores and their hair was in curls. The boys' socks were pulled up to their knees. None of them wore blue-and-white striped shirts. They waited with their fathers: SS men dressed in grey uniforms studded with skulls and swastikas. Nazi fathers smiling down at their rosy-cheeked children.

The kapo strode past the children, swung the gate open and walked into the ring. Alexander followed him, rearranging his face to hide his disappointment.

"Call them one at a time." The kapo leaned in to Alexander. "If the officers don't want you to touch their children, don't touch them. If they want you to lift their kid onto the saddle, do it. Don't talk to the children unless they talk to you. Don't smile at them unless they smile first. Don't ask their parents for money or food. You're invisible, unless they say otherwise." The kapo's voice was steely. "Got it?" He nodded at the first child waiting at the gate.

"Got it," Alexander said, his disappointment spiralling into fear. He turned to his first customer, wondering what the little girl's father had told her about the bald prisoner in the striped shirt.

She was four, maybe five, with red hair and lips that sat between dimples. She didn't talk to Alexander, or smile at him, just tugged on her father's arm until he hoisted her from the ground and settled her onto the pony. He stood beside her, his hand on her back, staring at Alexander. The helmet! Alexander had almost forgotten it. He lifted it from the fence post and passed it to the girl's father, who stood thin-lipped and silent on the other side of the pony. Alexander fed the reins through the girl's fingers with trembling hands. *You can lead a pony around a ring with your eyes closed, so quit shaking*, he berated himself. He squared his shoulders, lifted the lead rope and started to walk.

He didn't break into a jog like he did with Strudel, forcing Lili to bounce up and down in the saddle and shriek with excitement. He walked at a dull, even pace, once around the ring, the only sound keeping his footsteps company was the huffy breath of the pony and the crunch of her hooves. The birds were too hot to sing; even the crickets were silent in the sticky heat. The little girl's father lifted her off the pony, passed her a flask of water and carried her to a waiting car. Neither of them turned to thank Alexander.

A boy with buck teeth waited his turn by the gate. He was soft and round, his collared shirt stretched awkwardly over his belly, pink skin poking from between the buttons. Alexander wondered what he'd eaten for breakfast, a sausage perhaps or a runny fried egg with a thick wedge of bread to mop up the yolk. Alexander's stomach growled.

The buck-toothed boy lunged at Chestnut. "I want to get on by myself." He swatted his father's hand away.

"You heard my son." The officer turned on Alexander. "Help him." Alexander did as he was told. He bent down, locked his fingers together and peered up at the boy.

"Face the back of the pony." He softened his voice so it wouldn't sound like a command. "Now hold onto the horn and step into my hands with your left foot," he said, hoping the boy wouldn't be too heavy for him. The boy grabbed the horn with his fat fingers, lifted a pudgy leg and slid his foot into Alexander's cupped hands. Alexander braced himself. "Now spring off your right foot and swing your leg over the pony." Alexander looked across at the boy's father, saw the gun poking from its holster and the rubber baton hanging from his belt, and held his breath.

The boy settled into the saddle and Alexander breathed out. He picked up the lead rope and stepped forwards.

"My son wants to ride, not be led!" The officer stabbed Alexander's shoulder with his baton.

"Close your legs against the pony's sides." Alexander tried to raise his voice above a whisper. The boy squeezed his tubby legs around Chestnut's flanks and the pony began walking.

"I'm riding, Father. Look, I'm riding!" the boy shouted and Alexander felt relieved and angry at the same time.

"Well done!" he heard the father say. Alexander didn't need to turn and look at the man to guess that he was probably smiling across at his son, and that the buck-toothed boy was probably swollen with pride and smiling too. Alexander hated them for it. Hated himself a little too.

"Hurry up!"

Alexander turned at the sound of a voice and saw a young boy step from the line.

"It's hot and I'm thirsty and I'm tired of waiting."

The girl in front of him reached out a hand and grabbed the boy's shirt.

"We're all tired of waiting but I'm before you and you better not push in front or I'll tell my father."

The boy grumbled and slunk back into line.

They're tired of waiting, Alexander thought, returning to the gate with Chestnut. So am I. Seems all he'd done the last few years was wait. Wait for his father to return from his labour unit. Wait outside the synagogue to be marched into the ghetto. Wait to use the toilets, wait in line for meals, wait naked for the showers, wait to be tattooed. Alexander mopped his brow. Wait and hope that he'd be left alone so he could wait some more, because one day – Alexander bent low and clasped his fingers together – one day the Russians would come and the waiting would be over.

The buck-toothed boy hopped down and Alexander signalled for the next child. Her father waved her on.

"This way." He waved the young girl away from Chestnut's back end. He would've liked nothing more than to watch the pony step back onto her expensive leather sandals and crush her toes, but he needed the job.

"What's her name?" the girl asked, tapping Alexander on the shoulder.

"Chestnut," Alexander said. The girl had corn-coloured plaits and a smile as wide as a barn door. He couldn't look at her.

"Is she a pony or a baby horse?"

Alexander looked over at the girl's father. He was leaning on the gate, his face turned up to the sun, his eyes closed against the glare. Probably safest to answer her, he thought.

"She's a pony," he said, as he helped her onto the saddle.

The girl leaned forwards and waited for more. Alexander cleared his throat. He hadn't been asked his opinion in a long time. He barely spoke in full sentences any more, and when he did it was always in a whisper.

"You can tell because she has a thicker mane than a horse and a heavier coat." He ran a hand over Chestnut's red hair. "Ponies have shorter legs too," he said, looking into the girl's wide eyes. "And they're never taller than this." He let his hand hover just above Chestnut's head.

They circled the ring and the girl slid off the pony and took her father's hand. "Can we come back tomorrow, Papi, please?" she begged, pulling at her father's coat. The officer smiled and smoothed a wet slick of hair from her face. "I have to work tomorrow, *liebling*." He glanced at Alexander. "Say *danke* to the boy." He slipped his hand into his coat, took out a cigarette and offered it to Alexander.

Alexander didn't smoke. His grandfather had died two days before his sixtieth birthday, when Alexander was six. His mother had told him that it was the cigarettes that killed his *zaida* and that if she ever caught him with a cigarette in his mouth, she'd borrow his father's belt and pull him onto her knee, no matter how big he was. Alexander took the cigarette and slipped it into the rolled-up cuff of his trousers. Most of the men in the barrack smoked, the Rat included. It wouldn't hurt to have a cigarette up his sleeve. Or in his trouser cuff.

"Her name is Chestnut," he said to the next child, forgetting himself.

"I didn't ask you to talk," the boy's father said, lifting his child onto the pony. So Alexander didn't. He led Chestnut around the ring, slowly, and deposited the child at the gate. He then helped the next one on. And the next child and the next, until they all looked alike, and his shirt was wet with sweat and he was dizzy with hunger.

"Over here!" The kapo waved Alexander to the

stable door after the last child had left. "It's hot out there, give her a drink." He pointed to the water trough. Alexander hung the helmet on a fence post and led Chestnut to the metal trough. He shooed the flies from her eyes and watched her slurp the water, wishing he could touch his tongue to the wet metal. He hadn't been this thirsty in a long time. Not since the cattle train. When Chestnut raised her head from the trough and shook it, Alexander leaned in to catch the spray coming off her mane and when she stopped, and he saw the water drip from her nose, he reached out to catch it. He rubbed her wet neck and ran his hands over her soaking muzzle and brought both hands to his lips to suck the moisture from his fingers.

The men in the Horse Platoon filed out of the stable. In the harsh light Alexander could see their bruised skin and the dark circles under their eyes. Their shirts were stained blue-black at the armpits and their pants flecked with mud, but their horses' coats gleamed. The commander strode into the sunshine after them.

"Get to work! These horses need exercise. Run them around the paddock. I want to see them sweat." He raised his whip and brought it down hard against his boot. The men hurried into the yard, pulling their horses after them. The breeder's son, Nussbaum, left the stable last. He held his lead loosely, the commander's white stallion stepping into the sunshine after him. The horse's forelock had been combed back from his chiselled head and his feet were sponged clean. His muscles rippled. Alexander couldn't take his eyes off the horse. He watched them enter the paddock, wishing that it was his hand wrapped around the reins, his foot sliding into the stirrup. It wasn't fair, to be landed with the pony while the rest of the men – Isidor included – spent their days riding horses. Alexander gritted his teeth.

Nussbaum sprung off his right foot and raised himself up in the stirrup. The Horse Platoon fell silent. Men dropped reins, heads spun around. The kapo stiffened, backed away from the water trough and ran for the gate. Alexander watched him go, saw him lope into the paddock, lunge at Nussbaum and shout, "No!"

Alexander stared up at the boy who was frozen in ascent, having realized his mistake. No one else was on horseback.

"Get down!" the kapo hissed, clawing at the boy's pants. The boy swung his leg back over the horse but his foot didn't touch the ground.

"How dare you!" The commander's face twisted in anger. He grabbed Nussbaum by the collar, dragged him from the horse, yanked the boy's arm behind his back and marched him from the paddock.

"Tie him up and bring the rest of them." The commander stopped at an upright post sunk into the ground and shoved the boy onto his knees so that he kneeled before it. He kicked the boy's arms out and waited for a guard to tie his wrists to the post. Alexander felt winded. He'd thought the post was for tethering horses. He looped Chestnut's lead rope around a fence post and stepped into line. "Make sure they're watching." The commander turned to the inmates. "If anyone looks away, they get shot."

Alexander was going to have to watch. He dug his nails into his palms and forced his eyes to follow the sweep of the commander's boot. He saw the shiny black leather grow slick with blood, heard the crack of bone, saw bits of cloth cling to the heel. The breeder's son cried out every time the commander drove the boot into his back but the commander kept kicking until the boy's shirt hung in shreds and a river of dark blood leaked from his wounds, and then he kicked him some more. His face didn't grow plum-coloured with exertion or grow slack with the effort of breaking another man's bones. His face remained hard and unbending from the first kick to the last. Alexander watched it all with dry eyes, hypnotised by the commander's easy cruelty, aware that the men beside him were blinking away tears. *You're a brick wall*, he said to himself through gritted teeth. *Nothing gets through.*

The commander looked down at his boots. "I need someone to clean this." He stuck out a smeared shoe and crossed his arms over his chest. The kapo pointed at Alexander.

"But I don't have a..." Alexander meant to say rag, but a guard dragged him from the line and thrust him forwards. Alexander dropped to his knees in front of the commander and stared down at the man's boot. *Think*, he said to himself, rubbing his brow. His fingers skimmed the fabric of his cap, then closed over it. He pulled the hat from his head and dragged it across the commander's blood-spattered boot, back and forth until the leather gleamed.

The commander kicked Alexander's hand away, jerked his boot free and asked for his horse. Alexander shuffled back into line, pulling the sticky cap back onto his head.

"These are not your horses. You don't get to sit on them." The commander grabbed a handful of mane, shoved his foot into a stirrup and swung up onto his saddle. He glanced at Nussbaum, lying curled on the ground. "Your job is to feed, groom and exercise them." He paused. "And you do this by walking them to the paddock and letting them loose." He scanned the stablehands assembled before him. "Those of you who have served here for some time know your position. Riding is not part of the job." He ran his hand over his horse's flank. "You're lucky to be caring for such noble animals." He scanned the group. "You might learn something from them. Like hard work."

Alexander wanted to punch him between the eyes. He wanted to pull the commander's gun from his holster and aim a bullet through his head. Instead he was forced to watch the man circle the yard on his horse while Nussbaum bled.

"Send him back to Birkenau," he said eventually, sliding from his horse and pointing to Nussbaum.

Two guards dragged the boy to his feet and hauled him away.

The commander spun around and pointed to Alexander. "*He* can have Serafin."

Chapter 6

Serafin snorted and tossed his mane.

"You don't scare me," Alexander hissed, taking the reins and stepping into the stable. "You're a horse, and I know horses." He turned to the stallion. In truth he'd never worked with a creature quite as fine. His father's horses were good horses – strong, able, kind horses – but none of them looked like Serafin. None were as sleek and strong. None had a head as delicately chiselled or a coat quite as silken. Alexander reached out to pat the horse, to rub his neck and feel the velvet of his muzzle but before his fingers had even grazed Serafin's skin, the horse bared his teeth.

Alexander grabbed the reins and hurried to find the horse's stall, dragging the animal after him. The stall was easy to find; it was the one closest to the stable door and twice as large as the others. It was as big as his classroom back home. He bolted the door behind them and fell back against the hard wood.

"I'll cut you a deal. I won't pat you." He stared into Serafin's hard, grey eyes. "As long as you do as I say." He hoped to God the horse was smart. He could handle a cold horse but a dumb one would get him killed. "If the commander thinks I can't handle you..." He stepped towards the horse and blew three short puffs of air into his nostrils. Serafin's eyes widened. "OK," Alexander said, his breath slowing, "you recognize a greeting, that's good. You've got some smarts." He let the reins drop and walked slowly around the animal, grinning as Serafin's ears moved with him, tracking his footsteps. Alexander spread his fingers and placed them below the stallion's withers. He held his breath and pressed into the animal and, to his relief, Serafin pushed back against his hands. It was what smart horses did. Rather than pull away from, say a wolf clamped down on their leg, they moved into the pressure to lessen the risk of having their leg torn off. The stallion was smart. Alexander exhaled. Smart as his master, and just as icy.

He eyed the stallion suspiciously. He'd never been rebuffed by an animal before. Never known a horse to shy from affection. Still, there were worse things.

"I don't need you to like me," he whispered into the horse's ear. "I'm used to that." He straightened up and unlatched the door. "I just need you to behave." Alexander slipped from the stall to fetch a currycomb.

"Why's the pony still outside?" the kapo cornered Alexander by the grooming tray. Alexander opened his mouth. "I thought..."

"You're not here to think, you're here to work. You're responsible for two horses now. And neither of them must suffer. Finish up with Serafin and then attend to Chestnut." He stared at the currycomb in Alexander's hand. "After you groom the horses," he said, passing Alexander a bottle of shampoo and a bucket, "you'll want to muck out their stalls, top up the straw and clean their tack. Don't forget to polish the stirrup irons and brush the dirt from the reins. The saddle polish and rags are over there." He pointed to the far wall. "The other men can show you how to mix the feed. Best to prepare their dinner early. He pointed to a room which led off the stable. It's all in there." He turned to go.

"What about lunch?" Alexander asked, resting his chin on the top of the bucket, his arms straining under the weight of the bottles and buckets.

The kapo shook his head. "The horses are fed

twice a day, at six am and then at night, just before you leave."

"No. *My* lunch," Alexander blurted. The kapo stiffened and Alexander edged away from him, wishing he could rein his words back in. *Idiot! You've just seen a boy pummelled for slipping his foot into a stirrup. And now you talk back to a kapo?*

"Lunch is at noon." The kapo waved Alexander away with a calloused hand. "That's two hours away. If you get everything done, which I doubt... " He grabbed a sponge and dropped it into Alexander's bucket. "Then you can eat."

Alexander wasn't daunted by the long list of jobs. He'd grown up cleaning tack and mucking out stalls. He'd spent his summer patching fences and stacking hay bales and his winters shovelling snow. Every morning before school he'd collect the eggs from the chicken shed and haul the milk tubs to the house. He didn't mind hard work, he just didn't want to do it for *them*.

Alexander lifted the saddle from Serafin's back and ran a damp cloth over the leather. He'd dreamed of a place like this: a stable with a feed room, a tack room and dozens of stalls. He'd dreamed about owning one just like it with his friend Anton Hudak. Growing up on neighbouring farms, the boys had talked of little else. They'd planned their empire by the time they were twelve and found an abandoned paddock which they claimed as their own.

Over there, Anton would point at a patch of green, *will be the training arena.*

And there, Alexander would jump from his horse and walk to the fence, *will be the stables.*

Men would come from all over the country to have their horses tamed at the *Galloping Stallion Equestrian Park*. Alexander had even hammered two planks of wood together to make a sign, but he'd never hung it.

"I'll still do it," Alexander muttered. "And it will be bigger and better than anything I could've ever done with Anton." Alexander filled the bucket with water, dropped a bar of saddle soap into the tub and dipped a sponge into the filmy liquid. He wiped down the saddle and the reins, hung them up to dry and turned to the horse. Serafin's white hair was flecked with dirt.

"Let's get you clean," he said, grabbing the hard brush and running it over the horse's back.

Serafin snorted and stamped his feet.

"Keep still," Alexander said, pulling the brush through Serafin's tangled mane. "The sooner we get this done, the sooner we can eat."

Isidor poked his head over the stall wall.

"What makes you think he understands a word you say?"

Alexander ignored him.

"They're animals. They're stupid. If they had half a brain, they'd head for the hills."

"Stupid? The first time..." Alexander didn't have time for this; he had work to do. "Never mind." He took Serafin's head in his hands and sponged the stallion's face.

The first time he'd saddled Sari he'd found himself sprawled in the dirt with the saddle hanging upside down under the horse's belly. His father had laughed and told him that horses take a deep breath, just as you pull the straps tight. *They're smart*, his father had said, plucking the straw from Alexander's hair. *You have to pull the girth tight, and walk them around until they breathe out.*

There was a loud *thwack* and the wall dividing Alexander's stall from Isidor's shook violently.

"Keep it down!" a guard yelled from the other side of the stable. Alexander rose up on his toes and peered over the wall. Isidor was playing tug-of-war with his filly, trying unsuccessfully to pick up her foot to clean it. The horse struck out at the wall again, her pink nostrils flaring. She was a plain horse

79

with an honest face and Alexander wondered where the commander had found her and if there was a kid, on a farm somewhere in Poland, who had been forced to give her up.

"Let go of her foot," Alexander hissed. "You keep doing that and she'll start squealing and spook *all* the horses. Grab the hoof pick." He pointed to the curved tool lying on the floor of Isidor's stall. "Now gently pick up her foot." Isidor picked up the tool and reached for the filly's leg. "See that vee?" Alexander pointed to the soft pad abutting the top of the horseshoe. "Use the tip of the pick to remove the dirt that's caked in there. Pick it away from the heel towards the toe. You don't want to push any grit into the sensitive part of the foot. Good," he said. "Now set that foot down – easy, don't drop it – and move to the next one."

Alexander watched Isidor out of the corner of his eye. The boy was clumsy and clearly a novice, but he was gentle with the horse and did as he was told. "Now wipe her down. Watch me over the stall wall if you have to. You can copy what I do." Alexander left Isidor tugging at a clump of grass. The boy didn't deserve his help but the filly did. He turned to run a damp sponge over Serafin's neck. The horse stood stiffly, his neck taut; obedient but cold.

Alexander stifled a yawn. The air in the barn was warm and thick with the sweet smell of hay. Best get to work, he thought, mucking out the stall. He shovelled the dirty bedding into a wheelbarrow, checked the floor for loose nails and raked clean straw over the ground. Then he got to work on Chestnut.

"Serafin's getting impatient. He needs to eat." The kapo pulled Alexander from Chestnut's stall and marched him down the corridor. "This is where we keep the feed." He swung open a door and walked into a room lined with bins of grain and buckets of hay. A guard sat in the corner of the room, peeling an apple with a penknife. Alexander watched the curling peel fall to the floor.

"You have to soak the sugar beet for twelve hours before feeding it to a horse," the kapo said, grinding the apple skin into the dirt under the heel of his boot. "Carrots," he said, pointing to another container, as if Alexander had forgotten what real food looked like. Alexander stared at the impossibly orange carrots and then at the apples – whole apples, red and green apples, plump with juice – in a basket by the door. "The potatoes are over there." The kapo pointed to a full basket. Alexander stared longingly at the dirty brown vegetables. *Potatoes*. His stomach twisted.

"If anyone catches you with so much as an apple

core down your pants..." The kapo's face darkened.

"Of c-course," Alexander stammered, rushing to the corner of the room to grab a bucket. He plunged his hands into a bin, pulled out a handful of oats and tossed them into Serafin's feed bucket, feeling the grain slip through his hands before bringing his fingertips to his nose to inhale the scent.

"Don't even think about it." The kapo's voice was wintry. "If you eat your horse's feed, one of two things will happen. Either a guard will catch you and tie you to that whipping pole outside," he paused, his bushy eyebrows knitted together, "or your horse will lose weight, and you'll be tied to that whipping pole outside." He swung the door open. "Feed your horse. The commander will be here to ride him at two o'clock."

Alexander set the bucket down in front of Serafin and slipped back into the feed room to fetch a bucket of cool, clear water. He set the bucket of water down and waited for the horse to approach it, pleased that Serafin had left a smattering of oats and a beet at the bottom of the feed bucket. He bent over slowly and reached for the beet just as Serafin pulled his nose from the water and kicked out angrily.

"C'mon, you won't miss one handful," Alexander cooed, reaching towards the bucket. Arabians were desert horses, they could get by on scraps. The horse lashed out, his eyes bulging.

"The commander's got you trained but he's made you mean," Alexander said, escaping the stall. He supposed he could make Serafin warm to him eventually. A horse could be trained to do anything, with time and enough sugar. Alexander had time – he wasn't going anywhere – but he didn't have the energy. Serafin was obedient and would do as he was told. And that was more than enough. Becoming attached to the horse would only complicate things.

They didn't have to like each other.

Chapter 7

The lunch room was crowded with men bent over their bowls slurping soup. Some sat on chairs, others sat cross-legged on the cement floor sipping water from cups. The horses' feed room was crammed with buckets of vegetables and baskets of fruit. The lunch room was empty save for a metal cauldron sitting on top of a table, a splintered wooden ladle licked clean beside it and an empty pitcher.

Alexander had missed lunch. He found a chair and collapsed into it, distraught. There was plenty of hay in the stable. If the horses could eat it, he consoled himself, so could he. He'd work faster tomorrow and when the lunch whistle blew, he'd be first in line. He sat quietly and watched the men eat.

"There's still some left," the kapo grunted between mouthfuls of soup. He pushed his empty bowl aside and dragged another bowl to his chin. Alexander unclipped his cup from his belt and peered into the tureen. A puddle of grey soup lay at the bottom of the pot. It looked like the water in his mother's laundry bucket after she'd washed the floors, and smelled faintly of potato. He picked up the ladle, scooped out the remaining broth and slopped it into his cup.

At home, his mother had always given him the biggest portion. She liked to watch him eat, especially in those last weeks before they were sent to the ghetto, as if the act of filling his stomach might protect him from hunger later. He wondered where she was and hoped she had a job where she could skim a few potatoes from the bottom of a pot. Alexander's mother had earned a business degree when she was young, before she'd given up the city for life on the farm with her new husband. Her mind was sharp as a tack and that would help. And she hated to be idle. He couldn't remember a time when he'd returned home from school to find her sitting in the sun. She was either doing the books, ordering equipment, attending to dinner or milking the cows. *She'll be fine*, he thought, tipping the cup to his lips. *She'll be worrying about me.* He looked down at his stomach and saw that it was still caved in. He hadn't expected potato dumplings for lunch but he'd hoped for something more than he'd been fed in Birkenau.

With their hunger dampened, the talk in the room

turned to things other than food. The men around him talked of home and the end of the war and how they'd soon get to hold their wives and sweethearts. Girls were the furthest thing from Alexander's mind. And even if he did have someone waiting for him back in Košice, he sure as hell wasn't going to tell a bunch of strangers. Alexander had learned to keep his head down and his mouth shut. It was hard enough getting through each day without expending the extra energy required for conversation, so he sidestepped the banter, unless, of course, there was something to be gained.

"Commander Ziegler will be here in twenty minutes," the kapo called to him. "You need to be in the yard with Serafin in ten."

Alexander headed outside and found the toilets behind the stable – a slab of concrete with seven holes drilled into it, protected from the elements by a warped tin roof held up by four posts. There were no walls and no toilet paper, just a few strips of burlap torn from a sack, stuffed under a brick to keep the wind from carrying them off. It was the first time Alexander didn't have to share the toilets with anyone, but he wasn't alone. One of the stablehands was pulling weeds next to the toilet block. He looked up from the ground as Alexander lowered his pants, watched him for a few moments, then returned to his task.

"Two minutes!" the kapo called. Alexander gave Serafin a brisk brushing and lifted the commander's saddle onto his back.

"I need you outside!" the kapo shouted. Alexander grabbed a whip and brushed past Isidor who was trying, unsuccessfully, to unravel a lead line.

"Didn't you listen to Henryk's story?" Isidor reached for Alexander's whip. "We're not allowed…"

"I don't have time for stories." Alexander pushed him aside.

"Alex." Isidor's voice was tight. He wrapped his fingers around the whip and yanked it towards him.

"Not now," Alexander hissed.

"The whip." Isidor glared at Alexander. "You can't use it. We're not allowed to whip the horses."

"I need Serafin outside now," the kapo growled from the doorway.

Isidor pulled the whip from Alexander's damp hand. "Go," he whispered. "I'll put it back."

Alexander hurried outside and held out the reins.

The commander mounted Serafin, and lifted his hand in a Nazi salute. "Heil Hitler!" An SS Officer – the same man Alexander had seen at the gates of Auschwitz that morning – dismounted a black Arabian and returned the salute.

"Herr Hoess," the commander said, turning Serafin in a circle, "have you ever seen finer looking animals?" *Hoess* – the name ricocheted around Alexander's head. He knew that name. Of course. Alexander shuddered. Hoess was the commandant of Auschwitz and one of Hitler's highest ranking officers.

"All it takes is good breeding," Hoess said, offering the black Arabian a cube of sugar. "If we could only breed *people*," he glanced at Alexander, "the same way we breed horses."

Alexander drove his nails into his palms. It was a kind of hell having to stand there, in the baking heat, listening to them talk. Worse still, having to watch the commander close his legs against Serafin's sides and take off across the paddock. Alexander watched them go, the horse sliding into an easy gallop, his head held high and his white mane blazing. The commander rose in the stirrups and slid his gloved hands up the horse's neck as Serafin sailed over the first fence, his sleek coat snow-white against the deep green.

The man was an accomplished rider but Alexander knew he was the better horseman. The commander relied on the reins to control his horse; Alexander didn't need them. He'd taught himself to ride without reins, directing Sari with his legs, holding only her mane. Just a squeeze of his knees was enough to tell her what he needed. The commander seemed proud to be Serafin's master but their relationship would always be limited. Alexander would always be the better rider because when he sat on Sari, it was not as her master, but as her friend.

"*Neuer junge*, new boy." The kapo turned to Alexander. "You might want to do some weeding. The men whose jobs you took were shot because their horses ate poison brambles." He handed Alexander a trowel. "And keep an eye out for the commander. He'll expect you to be standing at the gate when he returns."

Alexander spent the rest of the afternoon shovelling horse dung and searching for poisonous plants. He pulled a clump of ragwort from the ground and burned the yellow flowers along with a handful of acorns. He worked beside men repairing fences and boys tussling over who would refill the water trough, hoping, perhaps, to sneak a drink when the guards' backs were turned.

The sun was already low in the sky when the commander returned from his ride. He slid from his horse and flung the reins at Alexander.

"Put him away for the night." He pulled a carrot from his jacket pocket and held it out for Alexander. "Here," he said. A dark smile crossed his face. "For the horse."

Alexander peeled the bridle from Serafin's head, and watched the carrot disappear between the horse's wet lips.

He had only just finished cleaning the tack when the kapo ordered the stablehands into the yard. The commander was waiting for them. "My whip. Get it for me," he snapped at Alexander.

But I've put Serafin away for the night, Alexander panicked. Why does he need his whip?

He ran to the stable, lifted the commander's black leather whip from its hook and returned with his head lowered and his arm outstretched.

Commander Ziegler ran his manicured hands over the black leather strap and began counting the men.

"One." He pointed his whip at the first man in line. "Two, three..." He stopped every so often to prod a man with his whip or fling a cap from someone's head in his search for stolen goods. Alexander glanced down at his trousers. The cigarette wasn't poking from the cuff but if he were forced to undress, it might fall out. Alexander had seen inmates smoking outside the barracks. Still, if the commandant found one on him ... anything could set the man off.

The sun dipped in the sky and the faces of the stablehands turned pink in the fading light. The guards sucked in lungfuls of smoke and the kapo chewed on his thumbnail.

"Twenty-two, twenty-three. Twenty-three!" the commander raised his voice and the boy next to Alexander lurched forwards.

"Not fast enough," the commander said, the tip of his whip sailing towards the boy's face and catching his skin. Alexander had never seen a whip used for anything other than training horses, he'd never thought of them as sinister.

"Twenty-four!" The commander pointed to Alexander and he leaped from the line.

"Twenty-five!" The commander stopped at Isidor and asked him to remove his shoes. The colour drained from Alexander's cheeks and he cursed himself for caring. Isidor pulled his boots off and turned his socks inside out. They were empty. The commander looked disappointed. He ordered the last boy in line to strip and shake his clothes out. The boy had thin arms and bow legs and his knees shook as he peeled off his trousers and shook them out.

The commander picked up the carrot that had fallen from the boy's pocket.

"Turn around," he said, a smile tugging on his lips.

The first strike of his whip left a red welt on the boy's back. The second split the boy's skin. He roared with pain like an animal caught in a trap but the commander didn't stop, not until the boy's back was slippery with blood. *That could've been me*, Alexander thought.

The commander disappeared into a shiny black car and two of the stablehands ran for a stretcher. They dragged the boy onto it, threw his clothes over his naked body and carried him to Auschwitz. The rest of the Horse Platoon followed in single file. Alexander's feet hurt. He longed for his bunk and the anaesthetic of sleep. But when the Horse Platoon stopped so the guards could light their cigarettes, the prisoners had to stand. Alexander peered at the boy on the stretcher. His clothes were wet with blood and his face was pale.

The familiar clash of cymbals signalled Alexander's return to Auschwitz. The sky glowed pink as the band welcomed the Horse Platoon back with a rousing march. Soot drifted through the air and settled on

Alexander's striped shirt, dusting his shoulders with black ash. No one talked about the sweet-smelling embers that fell day and night. Alexander wouldn't have minded so much, if remembering the dead meant picturing his sister riding her tricycle or sitting at the kitchen table eating butter biscuits. He wished he could remember her anywhere but on the cattle train, hungry and scared and tugging at his sleeve. He swept the ash from his shirt. He'd had nothing to give her. Not even a kind word.

He heard the familiar cry of *"Mutzen ab!"* and turned to face Herr Hoess. The kapo shouted, "Twenty-seven prisoners and one dead returning to camp," and the men lugging the stretcher laid it down before Hoess's scribe. The boy's shoes had already been stolen and his cup pulled from his belt. Alexander looked at the boy's empty eyes and wondered whether he could face another day in the camp. He'd seen men in Birkenau run at the electrified fences and thought them weak. Now he wondered if perhaps suicide wasn't an act of courage.

"Another dead?" Hoess smiled at the kapo appreciatively. "Good work."

Alexander walked through the deserted square, relieved to have missed roll-call. Isidor had told him on the long walk home that dinner at Auschwitz was a slice of bread, a sliver of sausage, a teaspoon of margarine and, on a good day, a piece of cheese. Alexander felt sick to his stomach but the spoonful of soup he'd swallowed at lunch hadn't filled the gnawing hole in his belly, so he stepped over the dead boy who'd been dumped by the door to line up for dinner.

"Welcome home." The Rat swung the door open. "I hope you boys aren't hungry." He bent his lips into a smile. Alexander scanned the dormitory. In the middle of the room, a bread knife lay on a wooden board scattered with crumbs. The air smelled of sausage. The Horse Platoon had missed roll-call but they'd also missed dinner.

Alexander stalked to his bunk. In Košice he'd done everything he could to avoid being trapped indoors. Outside meant open skies, endless fields and the possibility of escape. Inside, he'd felt caged. Now he *was* caged. If there was a means of escape Alexander would have taken it, but there was no escaping Auschwitz. He swore silently and tore off his shirt. If he wasn't going to get fed, he may as well get clean, he thought, taking off his boots and tramping to the shower. His fingernails were black and his mouth was dry and tasted foul. He stepped under the cool stream and showered off the sweat and horse hair. He held his face up to the needles and kept it there, happy that it hurt. He'd spent the day caring for a mean horse, grooming him for a man who whipped other men for pleasure. He'd spent the day making German children smile and their Nazi fathers proud.

He didn't deserve to eat.

Chapter 8

When he returned from the shower Alexander was surprised to find the barrack door open and most of the inmates outside. He stood at the door, watching them slip between the barracks, huddled in groups, talking and smoking. Isidor was standing among them, talking to a man bent over a cardboard box. He craned his head and saw Isidor reach into his pocket, pull out a cigarette and hand it to the man, accepting, in exchange, a package wrapped in wax paper.

"Excuse me." A bald man with bushy eyebrows tapped Alexander on the shoulder.

"We need one more to make up our minyan." The man's eyes slid towards the dead boy sprawled on the floor. Alexander shook his head. "Sorry, I—"

"You don't know what a minyan is. That's all right." The man pulled Alexander to the door. "We must hurry, before they come to take the body." He placed a hand on Alexander's shoulder to steady himself. "To pray for the dead, one must have ten Jewish men – a minyan." He stared up at Alexander with red-rimmed eyes. "God will watch over the dead if there's a minyan."

"God?" Alexander laughed out loud. "God's not here. Not in Auschwitz." Alexander shook the man's bony hand from his shoulder. "Besides," Alexander said, remembering his sister curled up like a question mark on the dirty floor of the cattle car, and his own unanswered prayers, "me and God aren't on speaking terms."

"Please," the old man begged, reaching for Alexander's hand. "He's my son."

"So pray for him." Alexander squirmed from the old man's grasp. "Because God sure as hell won't." The man's face crumpled and for a moment Alexander felt something almost akin to regret.

"Yitgadal v'yitkadash shmeh rabba." The old man shuffled towards the body, his head bowed.

Alexander covered his ears, but he could still make out the Hebrew words. His father had taught him the mourner's prayer the morning of his grandfather's funeral. He knew the next line the prisoners would chant – *Ye-hei shmei raba* – but he kept his mouth shut. He couldn't praise a god who took sons from their fathers, a god who forced men to watch their sons die.

* * *

Alexander sat on his bunk and pulled the cigarette the SS officer had given him from his trouser cuff. Isidor sat down beside him.

"You plan on smoking that?"

"Maybe." Alexander pocketed the cigarette. "Why?"

"Well, if you're not a smoker," Isidor said, taking the square of wax paper from his pocket, "and you were hungry, you could sell it for some of these." He unfolded the paper, pulled a pickle from it and slipped it into his mouth. "Or you could trade it for bread." He lowered his voice. "Your cigarette will buy you about a centimetre of bread at today's prices."

Alexander looked confused.

"The price fluctuates. If we haven't had bread for a few days, the price goes up," Isidor continued, "and a slice could cost you four cigarettes."

"Four cig—"

"We haven't got long – it's lights out soon – so shut up and I'll explain." Isidor bit into a pickle. "Cigarettes are the currency here. You can buy anything with them – socks, cutlery, a new coat. See the skinny guy with the big nose over there? That's Karpowski. He works in the warehouse where the guards dump the suitcases. He can get his hands on

98

a toothbrush, an extra blanket, a new pair of boots – whatever you need." Isidor slid the rest of the pickle into his mouth. "But if you just want bread, well, most of the guys in here would sell their left leg for a smoke. The Russians are mad for cigarettes. They'll hand over their *dinner* for a cigarette butt."

"But the guards?" Alexander cut in.

"The guards know. Where do you think they get their vodka from?"

"But the commander … the searches?"

"Zeigler knows how it works here. He wants us fed so we can work. He just doesn't want to *do* the feeding. The system works for everyone, as long as we don't rub it in their faces, so don't get caught trading," he finished at a gallop.

"I got lucky today." Alexander looked down at the cigarette in his hand. "Who knows when it'll happen again?"

"You really have no idea." Isidor shook his head. "Why do you think I lied to get in here? It wasn't for the showers." Isidor pulled the last pickle from its packaging. "Our platoon receives a distribution every week. Sometimes it's a handful of cigarettes, sometimes a whole packet." He licked the brine from the wax paper. "Of course, you have to pay off the guards and give the Rat his cut, but still…" He turned the paper over in his hands. "Reckon I can sell this." He slipped it into his pocket. "There's a huge market for toilet paper."

"Why are you telling me this?" Alexander asked, staring hard at Isidor. "We're even. I helped you with the horse and you took the whip off me. You don't owe me anything."

"I know." Isidor held Alexander's gaze. "I just figured … well, we're all in this together." He reached out to Alexander and Alexander flinched.

Isidor let his hand drop to his side. "You don't want friends. I get it," he said. "You help me with the horse, and I'll teach you what I know. Let's leave it at that."

The Rat swung his hammer at the dented hubcap, and the inmates dribbled back into the barrack to get ready for bed. Alexander pulled off his boots and went to climb onto his bunk when a withered hand wrapped around his ankle.

"A word?" Father Jablonski looked up at Alexander. The purple triangle stitched to his coat rose and fell with each laboured breath. He withdrew his hand and patted the bunk beside his. Alexander sat down and stared into the old man's face. His skin was as pale as the crumpled sheet he lay on. "Here," the priest rasped, holding out a veined hand to reveal a slab of grey bread and a piece of sausage. "I'm not going to eat it. *You* take it." Alexander wanted to snatch the bread from the priest's clammy hand before the old man changed his mind.

"I can't," he said instead, reaching out and closing Father Jablonski's fingers over his food, surprised by the warmth of the old man's papery skin. "You need to eat. This is not your battle."

"It's everyone's battle." The priest's voice was brittle.

"Well, if that's true," Alexander said, looking into the priest's colourless eyes, "then your best revenge is to survive this."

"I don't want revenge." The priest shook his head. "I want them to see the error of their ways." He held out the food.

"The error of their ways?" Alexander batted the bread away. "I just saw my commander whip a boy to death for stealing a carrot." His voice cracked. "They don't have a conscience. They don't feel guilt; they're not like us."

The priest smiled weakly. "They're exactly like us but they're given a gun and a uniform and orders they can hide behind." The priest turned his head to look at the guard standing in the doorway, hurrying the returning inmates towards their bunks with the butt of his rifle.

"Without that uniform on, he's just a bundle of straw," Father Jablonski whispered. "Take off his coat and he'd fall in a heap."

The room was still cast in shadow, and dawn a few hours off, when the Rat dragged in the coffee tureen and Alexander had his first cup of coffee. He sold his cigarette to a skinny Russian covered in scabs and drank his second cup, demanding the man's bread crusts as well, before handing it over. He felt full and it surprised him. He hadn't thought he'd ever feel full again and all it had taken was two cups of coffee and a few crusts of bread. Alexander ran his hands over his belly. He was full but his stomach felt uneasy. He'd sold nicotine to a dying man and taken his food.

The Horse Platoon entered the yard in the dark. Alexander smothered a yawn and followed the kapo into the stable. The air in the barn was warm and leathery-sweet and Alexander longed to sink into the straw beside Serafin and close his eyes.

"Commander Ziegler won't be riding today so you'll need to exercise Serafin after you feed and water him." The kapo followed Alexander into his stall. He clapped a hand on the stallion and Serafin rose to his feet. "And have Chestnut ready by the time the children arrive."

Serafin stamped his feet, impatient for breakfast.

"Get moving!" the kapo said.

Alexander grabbed a bucket and ran to fill it with water. He set it down heavily so that the contents splashed against the sides of the bucket and spilt over the edges, drenching his hands. He backed away from Serafin and sucked on his fingers, listening to the stallion lap the cool, clean water. He was a haughty horse but still Alexander longed to ride him. He wanted to be up in the saddle, the wind in his face, the blurred ground flashing under him.

Alone in the feed room with the door closed, Alexander mixed Serafin's feed. He'd just dug his hands into the bucket of oats, poured a fistful of grain into Serafin's bucket and a handful into his mouth, when he heard a squeal. The second cry was louder and, certain it came from a horse, Alexander grabbed the bucket and ran to Serafin's stall, relieved to see his nose still in the water bucket.

He ran between the stalls, peering into them as he passed each one until he glimpsed the horse who needed his help: a tall grey mare with swollen udders. He pushed past the men crowded around the stall door as she let out another high-pitched shriek.

"Don't!" Isidor grabbed Alexander's arm. "If anything goes wrong, you'll get blamed. Let *him* handle it." A stablehand stood by the mare's side. Alexander looked from the boy to his horse. Sweat streaked her swollen belly and she was breathing hard. He shrugged Isidor's arm away.

"Is she ready to deliver?" he asked the boy.

"I think so ... I don't know. I haven't done this before." The boy shrugged. The horse fell to her knees and rolled over onto the straw.

"Has a vet been called?" Alexander asked.

"Yes, but he's in Krakow. I don't think there's time."

Alexander ran through the list of all the things that could go wrong – the foal could be breech, it might be jammed or sitting sideways or too large for its mother. He had two choices. He could either get his hands dirty or walk back to Serafin's stall and shut the door. Walking away was smarter. It was safer. He'd promised his mother he'd make it back home. He'd promised Sari too. The mare's ears flicked in Alexander's direction. She was breathing hard. *You know what to do.* His father's voice snaked through his head. *You're a horseman. They can take your farm from you and your horses too, but they can't change who you are. You're a horseman and you can't let that horse die.*

Alexander wiped his forehead with the back of his hand and kneeled down beside the mare. The stablehand was crouched over her, running his hands over her muzzle, trying to quieten her. She lifted her head, looked at her flanks and flopped down again.

"She hasn't eaten since yesterday morning," the boy whispered.

"That's normal," Alexander said, pulling the boy from the horse and waving away the men who had gathered around the door. "She's getting close."

The boy shuffled to a corner of the stall and Alexander took his place beside the mare. He scratched her behind her ear and she nickered gently. When Sari had given birth to Paprika the spring before last, Alexander had stayed with her through the ninety-minute labour and sung to her. He couldn't sing in here and, even if he were allowed to, there was no song left in him. So he talked to her. He talked while she groaned and he whispered in her ear as her waters broke. He told her about the farm at 6 Gregor Lane as her legs stiffened and her belly contracted. He talked to her about milking cows and stacking hay bales and what it was like cutting through the woods on Sari's back.

He stopped talking when she started to push.

"Easy girl," he said, moving to the mare's hind

legs. He crouched beside her and as she shuddered, Alexander saw first one stick-thin leg wrapped in a white, filmy sack poke from her, then the other.

"What's wrong, why isn't it coming? Is it stuck?" The stablehand rushed at Alexander.

"Give her space." Alexander pushed the boy back. "She's resting, that's all."

Alexander paced the stall. He had to get back to Serafin and exercise the horse before the children arrived for their pony rides. As the light of dawn filtered through the windows, the mare pushed again and a nose and a head emerged followed by the foal's shoulders. Alexander shifted closer, tore the membrane away, grabbed the foal's spindly front feet and pulled out a slippery-wet colt, still attached to its mother's cord.

The stablehand flopped beside Alexander, his blue eyes watery.

"Watch the cord!" Alexander shooed him away, slipping his hands under the colt and shifting him closer to his mother. The mare lifted her sweat-streaked muzzle and ran a soft tongue over her baby's nose, before standing to sever the umbilical cord.

"Be sure to tell the vet to dip the foal's navel in iodine." Alexander beat back his joy at delivering the foal and turned for the door.

"Well, look at that!" The stablehand clapped his hands together and Alexander swung around. The colt was getting to his feet. He stood on his wobbly legs and took his first tentative steps.

"She'll want to suckle soon," Alexander said.

The foal stepped towards his mother, his mouth open at her teats, his legs splayed. Alexander peered over the stall door. The men had scattered and returned to their stalls. A single guard stood near the stable entrance, facing the yard.

"Guests first!" He pulled his cup from his belt and pushed the foal aside, wrapping his fingers around the mare's small pink teats. "There's plenty for both of us and the foal too, if we're not greedy." He squeezed the udder and peered into the cup. "The more we milk her the more she'll produce." His best friend Anton Hudak had sworn the stuff was better than cow's milk. He'd milked his plough horse on a dare and drunk a full cup. "You milk her in the morning and I'll take the afternoon." Alexander beckoned the boy closer. "Not more than half a cup each or the foal will go hungry and we'll be found out."

He tipped the cup up and drank the sweet milk, then waited for the boy to do the same. Alexander smiled as the boy finished his cup. They were in this together. Now that he'd drunk the milk, the boy couldn't turn him in.

By the time he got back to Serafin, it was too late to exercise him. Alexander bolted to Chestnut's stall, threw on her saddle and hurried outside. He'd have to come up with an excuse as to why he'd left Serafin indoors. Alexander scanned the yard. The guards sat in twos and threes drinking and playing cards. The kapo stood alone at the stable door, chewing on a piece of straw. Maybe no one had noticed...

Alexander lifted a little girl onto Chestnut's back and started around the ring. The pony's ears flicked back and forth, listening to her happy prattle. Alexander wished he could cover his ears. He didn't want to listen to her babble.

"What's your name?" she asked. Alexander pretended not to hear. "Your name?" she repeated. "I know Chestnut's name but I don't know yours. Mine's Danika. Danika Therese Hoch. Danika means morning star. Does your name mean anything?"

Alexander turned around. A wisp of blonde hair had escaped her braid and stuck to her forehead. She was wearing a white sundress, red patent leather sandals and white gloves, which she wrapped around the saddle horn. She reminded him of Lili.

"I don't have a name," Alexander said, turning away from her. Danika Therese Hoch laughed and her father looked up from his book.

"Alexander. My name's Alexander," he said to quiet her, regretting it as soon as she spoke his name.

"Hello, Alexander." She smiled, revealing a missing tooth.

Of course, she'd use my name. She's a child. She hasn't learned to hate.

Her face grew serious. "Tell me about this place."

"This place?" he said, looking nervously at the stable where her father sat.

"Yes." Her smile grew wide. "How many horses do you have? Do they know how to dance or do tricks? What do you feed them?"

Alexander offered her a tired smile. Twenty more steps and her turn would be over. "They eat carrots and apples."

"Father said I could bring Chestnut something next time. Should I bring him an apple or a carrot?"

"I prefer apples," Alexander said. "But ponies aren't fussy."

"Papi says *I'm* fussy." The little girl screwed up her face. "I hate vegetables." She laughed.

"What's so funny?" the girls' father said. He had come to the gate to help her from the pony. He reached into his pocket and drew out a cigarette.

"Oh, Papi." Danika laughed. "We were just talking about food. Alexander likes apples."

The officer's face paled. He shoved the cigarette back into his pocket and pulled his daughter from the pony.

Chapter 9

Alexander counted his cigarettes. Eight. He'd started with twelve but then the Rat had taken his cut and kept two for the kapo. But still – eight. Alexander held them up. "Karpowski," he called, waving the cigarettes in the air. "What do eight cigarettes buy me?"

"Oi!" Karpowski hurried towards Alexander, his cardboard box tucked under his arm. "Don't wave those around." He swiped Alexander's hand away. "Unless you want everyone here to know what you've got," he paused, "before they steal it."

Alexander lowered his hand and Karpowski sat down. "So, what do you need?" He smiled, wrinkles framing his mouth and eyes. "A toothbrush? Socks?" He rifled through the box.

"What's that?" Alexander asked, pointing to a yellow and white square of wax paper winking from under a bottle of vodka.

"That," Karpowski said, sidling closer to Alexander. "That's a krowki." He glanced at the cigarettes poking from Alexander's hand. "They're hard to get, very rare." He looked down at the cigarettes again.

"What's a krowki?" Alexander whispered.

"A krowki's a slice of heaven. It's fudge. It's very good." He lifted the wrapper from the basket. "You never had one?" Alexander shook his head, his eyes glued to the yellow and white paper.

"Normally I'd charge ten stubs." Karpowski's eyes slid to the cigarettes sweating in Alexander's hand. "But I see you only have eight, so, OK, take it for eight."

"Eight cigarettes?" Alexander could get a *whole* loaf of bread from the Russians for eight cigarettes. He looked over at Father Jablonski lying motionless on his bunk. The fool hadn't eaten for four days. He was as frail as a bird: his thin fingers, claws, his nose a beak on his narrow face. Alexander had offered him bread but it hadn't tempted him.

"Suit yourself," Karpowski said, swapping the candy for a wedge of cheese. He held the yellow block under Alexander's nose. "Doesn't taste as good, but it'll fill you up." The cheese smelled like old socks.

"No." Alexander pointed to the square of candy. "I want that."

112

He handed over his sweaty cigarettes, grabbed the fudge and rushed to the priest's bedside.

"Here," he said, pulling the wrapper from the sweet and holding it to the old man's lips. Father Jablonski looked up at Alexander with filmy eyes. "Child, you know I won't eat," he said quietly. "I want to do this. I'm ready."

The Rat struck the hubcap and Alexander hurried to his bunk, the square of fudge melting in his palm. Stubborn fool, he thought. God's not watching you. Neither is Hitler. Alexander slid the toffee between his lips. It smelled of vanilla and birthdays and tasted like summer. He sucked at its soft edges. There was butter, cream, milk and sugar – he could feel the grainy crystals with his tongue – and a hint of something burned and brown hidden inside. Alexander sucked hard. Caramel! He trapped it with his tongue and sucked the sweetness from it, wondering if Isidor would smell it on his breath.

He turned to face away from Isidor, touching the bunk alongside his with his foot and realized it was empty. Alexander reached out his hand and felt around in the dark. There was no one on the bunk next to him, or on the bunk next to that. He turned back to Isidor.

"There are men missing," he whispered into the

back of Isidor's stubbled head. "Why?"

Isidor turned around, slowly. "So, now you want to talk?"

"Yes." Alexander should have left it at that but he couldn't help himself; Isidor was so smug. "We have a deal. I help you with the horse and you tell me what you know. So what do you know?"

The Rat's door creaked open and a torch clicked on. Alexander held his breath and waited for the Rat to circle the room. When the footsteps receded Isidor raised himself onto an elbow and leaned over Alexander. His breath smelled of pickles.

"If the numbers don't add up when a work unit reports back to camp, Hoess makes the men wait outside until the numbers tally. If the men aren't back, it's because someone from their unit escaped."

Alexander lay in his bunk and waited for sleep. His lids snapped open when the barrack door swung ajar and the missing men filed in. He watched them climb onto their moonlit bunks and counted six beds still left empty.

The Rat swung his hammer at the dented hubcap to wake the men and Isidor opened his eyes.

"There are six empty beds," Alexander said.

Isidor sat up, threw off his sheet and swung his

legs over the bunk. "They've been shot."

"Who's been shot?" Alexander's eyes widened.

"The six men who used to sleep on those bunks."

"Why?" Alexander asked, not sure that he wanted to know.

"If someone escapes from a platoon, the guards shoot a couple of the men as punishment for the crime."

"And the escapee?" Alexander held his breath.

"The guards wouldn't allow the men back into the barrack unless they caught the guy."

"Is he here?" Alexander scanned the bunks.

Isidor shook his head. "You'll know who he is. They'll make sure of it."

Alexander watched from his bed as two men carrying a body between them lurched to the door. A sheet had been draped over the dead man. It wasn't the escapee. Alexander could make out the curve of the man's forehead and the slope of his nose under the fabric. Father Jablonski's arms hung loosely by his sides. His knuckles scraped the ground as the men bundled him through the door. Alexander felt a burning ache beneath his ribs. He'd seen dead bodies before, too many to count, but this was different. This was a man who'd chosen this place, chosen this fight. A man whose quiet body screamed out to God and the world to do right.

Alexander stared at the empty space where the priest had once lain. The straw mattress still held his shape and his coat lay folded at the end of the bed. Alexander touched the cool metal of the priest's silver cross. *Stupid man*, he cursed under his breath. *I offered to feed him. He didn't need to die. It's his own fault. His fault.* Alexander pulled his fingers from the cross. *Not mine.*

"Schema Israel Adonai Elohainu." Isidor stood beside Alexander and whispered the ancient prayer.

"Adonai Echod." A man in the next row answered his lament. They crawled down from their bunks and shuffled in from the bathroom, until there were twelve men huddled around the empty bunk.

"Hear o Israel, the Lord our God the Lord is one." Isidor took up the Mourners' Prayer. The Rat stood behind him, his head bowed. "In this hour of sorrow we give thanks for God's many mercies."

"Mercies?" Alexander grabbed the silver chain from the priest's bunk and flung it across the room. "What mercy did God show Jablonski?" He turned to the other men. "What mercy has he shown any of us?" Father Jablonski had died and taken God and hope with him. "There's no mercy, you fools." He stared at the men as if they were simple. "God's not looking out for us." He grabbed the priest's coat and stuffed it under his own pillow. "No one is."

"Has the pony been naughty?" Danika Therese Hoch sounded glum. They were halfway around the ring and Alexander hadn't yet turned to greet her. "You haven't said one word to me, so either Chestnut's made you grumpy or I have."

"I'm not angry," Alexander said, staring at the ground. He was too exhausted to be angry. Too worn down by watching men die.

"Well, I am," she said, tugging on the reins to slow Chestnut. Alexander turned around. Her eyes were red and her skin was blotchy. Alexander looked over at the girl's father. He was resting under the shade of a silver birch, his nose in a book. He mustn't see her frown. She was here to ride ponies and have a good time.

"Papi's sending me away," she hiccupped, "to live with my aunt in Berlin!" She pulled a lace handkerchief from her skirt pocket and blew her nose. "He says this is no place for children." She looked at Alexander and he saw in her face the same sadness and confusion he'd seen in his sister's face the day they were loaded into the cattle cars. He'd lied to Lili that day, when she asked him why the

Hungarian police were locking the doors. *To keep us safe*, he'd said. Safe.

"He's right," Alexander said. "This is no place for kids."

"He didn't want me to come today," she continued, blowing her nose loudly. "But I *made* him bring me." She waited for Alexander to say something. "I had to say goodbye to Chestnut, and to you." She rushed to fill the silence but Alexander wasn't listening to her any more. He was thinking about Max, who'd said their friendship was too dangerous, and Hilde who'd looked through him when they passed each other on the street and Martin who'd told him not to come over any more, and Anton—

Alexander pressed his nails into his palms until they carved perfect moons. Anton, his best friend who'd called him a Christ-killer and spat in his face. Loneliness and self-pity tapped him on the shoulder but Alexander swatted them away. He was better off without Danika Therese Hoch. Better off without all of them.

He lifted her from the pony's back and set her down on the ground. The little girl threw her arms around Chestnut. "It's not fair," she said, planting a kiss on her dusty neck. "I want to stay."

Alexander peeled her from the pony. "You'll be

fine," he muttered, pulling his hand from hers. She had small fingers, like his sister, the same tear-stained blue eyes, and the same pout. Alexander looked down at her. He couldn't hate her. He hated her father and Hitler and himself a little too, for being a Jew, but not Danika Therese Hoch. "You'll be fine," he said softly. "Goodbye, Danika."

He returned Chestnut to her stall and followed Isidor to the lunch room where the kapo was standing over the tureen, spooning soup into bowls. He filled three for himself, then rolled up his sleeves and plunged his hairy hands into the pot. He fished out a potato and dropped it into the first bowl and added a carrot to the second.

"Next!" he shouted.

Alexander held up his cup but he wanted more than watery soup. Now that he'd tasted fudge, he wanted pickles and cheese, and marmalade for his bread.

He gulped down the soup, left the lunch room and slunk to where the riding equipment was kept. He scanned the back wall for things he could sneak into the barrack to trade for food. The feedbags could be picked apart at the seams and sold as cloth, the saddle pads could double as pillows and the lead lines could be cut into strips and sold as belts or bootlaces. With all this stuff he didn't need Karpowski; with all this equipment he could fill his own cardboard box. Alexander picked a currycomb from the grooming tray. Beside it was a pair of clippers for trimming hooves. He wondered what the going rate for nail clippers was: a loaf of bread, at least. If only there was a way to avoid the commander's nightly search.

Isidor took a brush from the grooming tray and yawned.

"Heinz!" A guard with thinning red hair and a face ravaged by scars called to the kapo. "One of your Jews is falling asleep on the job." Isidor froze mid-yawn.

"You tired?" The guard stepped in front of him. "You want to sleep?" He pulled his truncheon from his belt. "I can put you to sleep." He jabbed the baton at Isidor's chest.

"You boys have *all* the fun." The kapo slid between Isidor and the guard. "How about giving me this one? I've been waiting to teach him a lesson." He elbowed Isidor in the stomach and the boy doubled over. The guard's mouth curled upwards.

"Why not?" he said, stuffing his truncheon back into his belt. "Be my guest."

The kapo nodded his thanks, grabbed Isidor by

the shirt collar and dragged him to his stall, kicking the door shut behind them.

"Get to work!" the guard spat at Alexander before buttoning his coat and stalking outside.

"He was a good kid." The man next to Alexander said.

"What do you mean *was*?" Alexander stared after Isidor.

"Well, he's in there with the Butcher..." The man chose a currycomb from the grooming tray and turned to leave.

"The Butcher?" Alexander called after him.

"Yeah, the Butcher." The man stopped. "He worked in an abattoir. Before they put him away for murder. Ten years. They say he used a meat cleaver."

Alexander ran to his stall and squeezed past Serafin – who snorted at the intrusion. *The kapo has a shaved head like me*, Alexander thought, pressing his ear to the wall. *He wears a yellow star.* Alexander searched for an explanation, a reason why the kapo would ask to beat Isidor. The wall shook and Serafin pricked his ears trying to make sense of the grunting sounds. Alexander heard the sound of a piece of wood swung hard against flesh. Something slammed into the wall, Isidor cried out, there was a long silence, then the sound of snapping twigs.

Alexander clapped his hands over his ears and slid down the wall till he was sitting on the straw with his knees drawn up to his face. Pain snaked through his head. He wished the wall separating his stall from Isidor's was made of stone so he couldn't feel it judder every time the boy slammed into it. He pictured Isidor bleeding on the other side of the wall and he hated himself for wondering if he'd be the kapo's next victim, instead of scaling the wall to help the boy. Alexander sat in the festering silence. Isidor wants to be my friend. He shook his head. I don't have the first clue about how to be a friend.

Chapter 10

Alexander watched Isidor stumble from the stable, a bloodied knee poking from his torn trousers, his face streaked with dirt. A slashing line ran across the bridge of his nose and his left eye was swollen shut. He looked like he'd been run over by a tractor. He hobbled into line and stood, eyes downcast, as the commander prodded the men in search of a lump of sugar or a stale vegetable, any excuse to cull the herd.

Isador limped back to Auschwitz behind Alexander. When they neared the checkpoint he pointed to the main gate. A man stood just in front of the entrance, dressed in black tails and a top hat. He wasn't a musician. Alexander had seen him in the barrack before – a tall, lean man with black eyes and pale skin, except that one of his eyes was purple now and the skin on his cheekbones was bruised and swollen. He stood with his hands tied behind his back, a cardboard sign strung around his neck.

"That's him," Isidor said. "The escapee from last night."

Alexander narrowed his eyes as he approached the gate to read the words scrawled across the placard hanging from the man's neck: *Hurray, I'm back.*

The guards dispersed as soon as they were inside the main gate, leaving the kapo to deliver his work platoon to the Rat. Isidor had slowed the men's march and the lights were already out when the Rat ushered them through the door.

"Do you need help getting up to your bunk?" one of the men in the Horse Platoon, whose name Alexander didn't know or care to know, whispered in Isidor's ear.

"I'm fine," Alexander heard Isidor say, before catapulting himself onto his bed.

"But your leg…" Alexander stammered, climbing up after him.

"The leg's fine," Isidor said. "It's just a scratch."

A *scratch*? Alexander remembered the walls shaking and the sound of snapping bones.

"The kapo's all right." Isidor brought his mouth to Alexander's ear. "The blood is just for show."

"I don't understand," Alexander said. "They call him the Butcher."

"A rumour he started himself."

124

"Himself?"

"Look," Isidor said, growing serious, "you can't let on."

"So the kapo's on our side?" Alexander ventured.

"I suppose so." Isidor pulled off his boots and lay down. "Sometimes, when the guards are watching, he has to break a nose, but if he can get away with it, he'll leave you alone. It's a shitty position to be in."

"What do you mean?" Alexander grew confused. The kapo got three bowls of soup and didn't have to work.

"He can't put a foot wrong. If he does, he'll be stripped of his position and sent back to the barrack."

"To live like the rest of us," Alexander huffed.

"No, not like the rest of us," Isidor said. "The previous kapo who was stripped of his rank lasted one day in his old barrack. His men beat him to death his first night back."

Alexander woke at midnight, clutching his stomach. *No*, he thought, gritting his teeth. *I can't get sick. I can't.* He tried to sit up, but the pain tore at his belly and he fell back onto the bed. He'd been thrown from a horse and had the stuffing knocked out of him in fights that weren't fair, but nothing that felt like this. Searing pain like a red hot poker shoved through his guts. He stuffed a corner of his blanket into his mouth to stop himself from crying out and hugged his stomach.

He had to get to the toilet. Maybe if he got to the toilet, he could rid himself of this bug gnawing at his insides. He dragged himself onto his elbows and sat up when it hit him again, a wave of blistering pain deep in his belly. He breathed through it, slid off the bunk and stumbled to the toilet in the dark, but he was too late.

He lay on the bathroom floor, his pants around his ankles in a puddle. If any of the inmates walked in, he was done for. He was sick and the men couldn't afford to have him – or his infection – anywhere near them. They'd take one look at him lying on the floor in his own shit and dump him at the infirmary. He couldn't blame them, he'd do the same. He crawled to the sink and turned on the tap. They wouldn't give him medicine at the infirmary, they'd give him a bed, and let him lie there, rot there, till the SS came to empty the room. It wasn't a hospital, it was a waiting room for the crematoria. A one-way street.

Alexander peeled off his pants, threw them into the sink and washed the muck from them while his stomach churned. No one must know. He kneeled down and wiped the mess from the tiles, rinsed his pants out again and wiped himself down. No one.

He dragged himself to a toilet, slumped down on the cold seat and wrapped his arms around his stomach. When he was sure there was nothing left inside him, he stepped into his wet pants and made his way back to his bunk by the moon's bluish light. His stomach still hurt but the cramps had settled to a dull ache. If I can just get a few hours sleep, he convinced himself, I'll manage the hike – and the horses – and it won't be the last time I get to see the stars or the moon…

"Alex! Wake up!"

Alexander opened his eyes and saw Isidor bent over him, his face creased with concern.

"I'm up." He swatted Isidor's hand away.

"You look like hell."

"I'm fine." Alexander forced his lips into a smile. "See?" He climbed from his bunk, stood for a moment, then ran for the bathroom.

"I heard you get up last night." Isidor came into the bathroom. "Can you get off the toilet?"

Alexander's stomach bug bared its teeth. "Just give me a minute." The bug sank its teeth in and Alexander doubled over.

Isidor ran from the bathroom.

"Isi! No!" Alexander tried to stop him but it was too late. He'd gone.

Get up, Alexander told himself, gripping the toilet bowl with both hands. "Get up and walk out of here." But he couldn't. When he tried to stand his legs felt hollow and the room spun. He slumped over the toilet and buried his head in his hands.

"Here." Isidor shoved a heaped teaspoon under his nose. Alexander blinked at the gelatinous lump.

"What is it?"

"Something to stop the diarrhoea."

Alexander brought the rusted spoon to his lips and swallowed the white paste. It tasted like raw dough.

"You should skip lunch for a few days." Isidor helped him from the toilet. "No soup, just coffee and bread."

"Where did you get that medicine?" Alexander asked, wincing. "I might need some more." He wrapped his arms around his belly. He wanted to fall into bed. Instead he was standing outside the barrack, waiting for the Rat's order to march out.

"I know someone," Isidor whispered. "Joseph Bauman from the Field Platoon, four beds up from us." He swatted Alexander's hand from his stomach – the guards were circling.

"Where does he get it?" Alexander spoke quickly.

128

"There's a man. A farmer. He hides things under the hay bales for the inmates sometimes. Medicine, fruit – he hid a skinned rabbit once."

"What will another spoonful cost me?"

"Sugar cubes," Isidor said. "Or cigarettes. You got any?"

Alexander shook his head.

"Something wrong with you?" The kapo followed Alexander into the stable. "You sick?" He grabbed Alexander's shoulder and spun him around.

"No, I'm fine," Alexander stammered. He broke away and hurried towards Serafin's stall. "I just had to go outside to get…" *What?* Alexander panicked. His head was still foggy with pain. *What did I have to get?*

The kapo was right behind him. There was nowhere Alexander could go.

"Because if you're sick," the kapo brought his stubbled face close to Alexander's, "I can get someone else to take Chestnut out."

"No." Alexander shook his head frantically. No, I can't lose this job. "No, I'm—" He searched for the right words. The kapo held up his hand to silence him.

"I can get someone else to do your work," he lowered his voice, "and you can help Goldberg shoe horses out the back. Near the toilets." His eyes drifted to the back wall where a guard stood, watching them.

"No arguments!" he shouted. He grabbed Alexander by the collar and dragged him past the guard, shoving him roughly. "Outside! Now!"

The blue day turned to black night.

"You never said thank you," Isidor whispered into the dark as the men returned to the camp.

"What for?" Alexander asked.

"For the medicine." Isidor walked past the checkpoint and into the barrack. "You never thanked me. I'm the only one here who still speaks to you. Or haven't you noticed?" Isidor shook his head. "Forget it."

"Good," Alexander shot back, "because I'm not expecting you to thank me every time I step aside to let you watch me groom or tack my horse. This works. For both of us." Alexander followed Isidor through the barrack door and crawled onto his bunk. The medicine had stopped him running to the toilet but his stomach still felt bruised and his skin was clammy. "So, how did you get the sugar past the commander to pay Bauman for the medicine?" Alexander asked without apology.

Isidor climbed up beside him. "Give me your shirt."

"What?" Alexander sat up. "You won't tell me unless I give you my shirt? Go to hell."

Isidor rolled his eyes. "You want to find out how I smuggled the sugar cubes?"

"I'm not giving you my shirt." Alexander glared at him.

"Fine." Isidor's fingers flew to his collar. He undid the first three buttons to reveal a secret pocket sewn into the lining. "Come with me."

Alexander hurried after him to the barrack next door. It was identical to theirs, same kennel-smell and grimy walls, same decaying bodies and dirty bunks. Isidor stopped to shake an old man's hand.

"Jeno Weisz meet Alexander..." Isidor hesitated. "Alexander..."

"Altmann." Alexander stepped from the shadows and shook the man's hand.

"What do you need?" the old man said. He took a length of cotton from his trouser pocket.

"What do I need?" *I need a meal. I need a doctor. I need to go home.*

"You need a hole patched?" He fingered Alexander's frayed shirt.

"Jeno's a tailor. He used to make three-piece suits," Isidor explained. "Now he works the machines making uniforms for the SS."

"Ah, he wants a pocket." The tailor nodded, unbuttoning Alexander's shirt with his spidery fingers. "I can get this fabric." He opened the shirt and ran a crooked forefinger along the seam. "And if we stitch it here, no one will see it."

He let the shirt fall and Alexander remembered his mother hunched over her sewing machine, stitching gold coins into the lining of her warm winter coat the night before they were marched into the ghetto. She'd already sewn her engagement ring into the hem and two gold chains into the shoulder pads.

"It'll cost you." The man held his hand out. "What d'ya got?"

"Nothing right now." Alexander buttoned his shirt. "But I can get you some cigarettes in a few days."

The old man grinned. "I want ten."

"Seven." Isidor grabbed Alexander's shirtsleeve and pulled him to the door. "The same as you charged me."

Chapter 11

Alexander made it through the next day, fell onto his bunk ragged with exhaustion, and woke the next morning to do it all again. He forced himself to smile at the SS children and help them onto Chestnut's back. He fed and exercised Serafin, groomed the horses, cleaned their saddles and mucked out their stalls, day after day until the days folded into each other and turned into weeks.

Summer slipped into autumn and the leaves on the birch trees turned orange. The heat lost its intensity, the days grew shorter and Alexander lost track of time. He turned fifteen on one of those pale autumn days but he wasn't sure which. It didn't matter. All that mattered was that he got through the day, did his job, avoided trouble and stayed away from Birkenau where death lurked, waiting to pounce.

The fate of his parents robbed him of sleep and his sister's last days haunted his waking hours, but the knot of hunger in his belly loosened as he grew more adept at stealing. He took what he could, stuffing a clump of oats into his mouth for every fistful he threw into the feed bucket and slipping potato peel into his secret pocket when he could. He milked the mare and traded cigarettes for bread and cheese, refusing to become entangled in the other men's lives. He was hungry and his thin arms hung from his narrow shoulders, and his kneecaps poked from his spindly legs, but he wasn't the thinnest. He wasn't as thin as the men whose food he devoured – the men who bought his cigarettes, the men the SS plucked from their bunks and marched away. Alexander watched them go, these men who he poisoned with his cigarettes. I can't force them to stop smoking, he thought, and I'm not going to feel guilty about giving them what they want. It's not up to me whether they live or die.

The commander stayed angry. There were days he would come into the stable just to whip them. He'd pick one of the stablehands, invent a minor offence – a horse looked tired, a mane wasn't brushed – and whip the boy with his crop, the black lash cracking like a rifle. It was just a matter of time before it was Alexander's turn.

He refused to think about it. Refused to think about dying – or living – because he was afraid of both. *Just get through the day*, he told himself. *Focus on the horses.*

He tried. He ignored the ground when it shook and the sky full of planes and the men's whispered talk of advancing Soviet troops, because the next day the sky would be empty and nothing had changed, and nothing ever would. Alexander kept his eyes and ears open and his heart shut. He batted away any talk of the future and tried to let go of the past. But every so often, in the quiet spaces between shampooing and brushing, and during the long marches, his memories got the better of him. He caught himself daydreaming about his mother's coal black eyes and his father's curling moustache. He didn't allow himself to return home too often, but sometimes the memory of his sister's laugh or the soft skin of Paprika's nose clawed its way into his head and he'd sit with the past for a while before beating the memory back.

He was thinking of home as he waited for the commander to return from a day-long ride, when Serafin loped into the yard, his head hanging lower than usual.

"Did you check Serafin this morning?" The commander slid from the stallion's back. Alexander took the reins and nodded.

"Something's off. He didn't want to take the jumps."

Alexander's eyes drifted from the commander's whip to the horse's torn shoulders.

"I want him fixed." The commander's voice blistered with anger.

Alexander led Serafin to his stall. He peeled the bridle from his head and Serafin groaned.

"OK," Alexander said, pressing his fingers to the horse's neck, "let's check you out." Serafin's pulse was racing. "What's wrong with you, boy?" The horse's eyes were cloudy and his skin was slick with sweat. Alexander panicked. Had he missed something this morning while grooming the horse? Was there a crack in his foot which he'd left unattended? A wound that had become infected? Alexander picked up each of Serafin's feet and scraped the mud from his hooves. They looked strong and healthy. No swelling. No cuts, bruises, puncture wounds or cracks. He ran his hands over the horse's legs. They weren't swollen, tender or hot to the touch.

"What's wrong, boy?" Alexander asked, sponging clean water into Serafin's mouth.

The horse licked the drops from his lips.

Then he dropped like a stone.

Alexander stood over him, sweat beading his

136

forehead. The horse lay on the ground, his silver flanks dirty with straw. His tongue hung from his mouth and his breath was rasping.

"Get up!" Alexander shoved him, but the horse lay like a dead weight.

"The commander will be here soon." Alexander dropped onto his knees. "Get up!"

Serafin closed his eyes.

"No, don't do that, don't go to sleep. Here, eat something." Alexander grabbed a fistful of straw and held it to the horse's lips.

Serafin thrashed his legs but he couldn't stand. He lifted his head to look at Alexander.

"Everything will be OK." Alexander's shoulders slumped. He stared at Serafin. If he wanted to help the horse, he'd have to think like a horse. Alexander preferred to be left alone when he was ill – left alone in general. "That's because I'm not a herd animal," he said to himself. "I don't need anyone to protect me; I can take care of myself."

If he *was* a herd animal, he'd want someone to protect him. Alexander lay down next to Serafin and smoothed his back. He thought of all the sounds horses make: the nickers, whinnies, whickers and snorts, and tried to fill the silence with a comforting voice.

"I'll look after you," he whispered into the horse's ear. "You'll feel better soon." Alexander buried his face in Serafin's mane. "This will all be over soon and before you know it you'll be going home." He ran his calloused hands over Serafin's muzzle, watched his laboured breathing for a few moments, stood up reluctantly and walked to the door.

He found the kapo in the feed room.

"Call the vet. Serafin needs to be seen," Alexander forced the words out.

The kapo lumbered towards him. "You sure?" he said, his words a warning.

Alexander nodded. He knew that the last stablehand to be responsible for Serafin had been shot because the horse had a stomach-ache. He knew that as soon as the kapo hung up from the vet, he'd call the commander.

"I'm sure," he said softly.

Alexander scrambled to the back wall as the vet, a lanky man with a shock of curly hair, entered the stall, followed by the commander. He pulled a stethoscope from a battered black bag and pressed it to Serafin's heart. Alexander stood in the corner, a drum beating in his chest.

"Aren't you going to check his feet?" the

commander asked. "These boys have no idea how to shoe horses or maintain their feet."

The vet pressed an arthritic finger to his lips and closed his eyes as he swept the stethoscope over the horse's chest. The stall was quiet except for the horse's heavy breathing.

"It's his heart." The vet lowered his stethoscope.

"What do you mean *his heart*?" The commander reeled back from the horse.

"He has a murmur."

A murmur. Alexander remembered his father pressing his ear to one of the new colts and declaring him healthy. He had a murmur, his father had told him, a beat between the normal heart sounds. Most healthy horses had a murmur of one sort or another.

"In some cases," the vet folded the stethoscope into his bag, "the heart murmur is an indication of a malfunctioning heart. In other cases, it has no health significance at all."

"Which is it?" the commander thundered. The vet's mouth grew pinched and Alexander retreated deeper into the corner, ovals of sweat under his arms.

"In this case, I believe, it's a serious heart problem." He looked down at the horse. "Serafin's heart valve is leaking."

"Are you certain?" The commander's mouth twisted in disgust.

The vet nodded.

"Has it always leaked? Or is it something that happened recently?" The commander directed his words at the vet but he was looking at Alexander. "Is it something that could have been prevented?"

Alexander stiffened. He stared at the vet, waiting for him to answer, willing him to say it wasn't his fault. *Say it*, Alexander begged silently. *Say it's not my fault.*

"These things happen." The vet looked uncomfortable. "There's no one to blame. He's probably had the condition since birth. All it means," the vet measured his words, "is that he can't be exercised too strenuously."

Alexander flushed with relief. If Serafin's condition was anyone's fault, it was the commander's for pushing him too hard.

"So you're saying I can't take him up to a gallop? No jumping fences? No races?" The commander stared at the vet.

"Not if you don't want his heart to fail." The vet stood up. "Main thing is, Serafin will be fine. With rest, he has every chance of surviving this. He'll need—"

"So, the officer who recommended this wreck of a horse misled me." The commander spoke in a low voice, his mouth tight with anger. "I was promised a perfect specimen, a horse with a perfect pedigree. I was promised champion lineage." He prodded Serafin with his boot. "Not this." His lip curled as though he'd just bit into a lemon.

The horse groaned.

"Shall we step outside?" The vet took the commander's arm and nervously steered him to the door. "There are medications we can discuss." The door slammed shut behind them.

Alexander slipped from the shadows to stroke Serafin's neck. The commander and the vet continued their exchange on the other side of the stall wall. Alexander could hear only snippets of their muted conversation, strings of words, nothing he could hold onto.

"Everything's going to be fine," Alexander said and Serafin's eyes fluttered open. He pulled a blanket from the shelf, draped it over the horse and lay down beside him, nose to nose.

Alexander was bent over the horse, sponging the sweat from his flanks when the door swung open. He looked up and saw two sets of boots.

"Shoot him!" the commander hissed.

The kapo's forehead wrinkled in confusion.

"Did I not make myself clear?" Commander Ziegler pulled out his gun. "I want you to shoot him."

Alexander's mouth flew open. He wanted to shout *It's not my fault!* but the words wouldn't come. *I don't want to die.* He tore at his skin of his palms. *Not yet. Not until my father comes home. Not until my mother* … His eyes pooled. His mother. He'd promised her he'd make it back home to Košice.

A muscle twitched in the kapo's bony jaw.

"You want me to shoot him now? Here?"

The commander nodded. "I hear you have experience with this type of thing." He sneered at the kapo. Alexander's heart thrummed in his chest.

"Good. It's settled then." The commander slid his gun back into its holster. "You'll shoot the horse and dispose of its corpse."

Shoot the horse? Alexander breathed out. The horse! He felt sick with relief, dizzy with it. Serafin was to die. Not him! Relief flooded his body. Relief, then shame. He was a horseman. He didn't like Serafin any more than the commander did, but he was a horseman, like his father and Serafin didn't need to die.

"What if I take care of him?" The words escaped Alexander's mouth before he could stop them.

"What was that?" The commander's mood darkened. The kapo stood behind him, shaking his head.

Alexander cursed himself. He should have shut up. But he'd done that once. He'd stared into Paprika's sad face and handed Sari's filly over to the Hungarian police without a fight. The ropes reining in Alexander's past snapped and the memory of the police storming his farm, demanding horses, hurtled towards him.

Saving Serafin won't make up for what you did to Paprika, he thought, or what you said to Lili when she staggered from the cattle train.

"I could look after him," he continued, half-heartedly. "He could still be of use. The children could ride him. They're always after me to put them on a horse." Alexander's voice trailed away.

"I want him shot." The commander brought his face so close to Alexander's, the boy could smell his breakfast. "I can't abide bad breeding." He stepped away from Alexander, looking him up and down, as if seeing him for the first time. "And since you're so fond of the horse, and so concerned to do this right," the commander's face relaxed into a smile, "*you* shoot him."

Chapter 12

The kapo followed the commander from the stall, leaving Alexander alone with Serafin. Alexander slumped onto the straw. He could feel Serafin's steaming breath on his skin. The horse lay beside him, his head flat on the ground, his tail fanned out behind him. Alexander felt the tears start. *Stop it!* he said to himself. *You were stupid to have grown fond of him. Stupid and weak.* Alexander wished he were made of stone – cold hard stone – instead of thin skin and a feeble heart. *You've gone soft.* He stood up and shook the straw from his clothes. *And that's precisely why you should shoot him.*

He turned to Serafin. He'd never shot an animal before. He'd killed a rabbit once, on a dare. Did it with a slingshot and a sharp rock. Anton had congratulated him, but Alexander had returned to the soggy patch of grass later that day to bury the animal.

The door creaked open.

"Let's get this over with," the kapo grumbled, pulling a pistol from his coat pocket and holding it out for Alexander. The gun was black, its polished barrel gleaming in the fractured light. It was the same type of gun the guards used to taunt the inmates, the same gun they exploded into heads and chests. Alexander stared at the long black muzzle.

"A bullet between the eyes should do the job." The kapo pressed the gun into Alexander's hand and pointed another at his head. "This one's in case you get any smart ideas."

Alexander wrapped his trembling fingers around the grip and turned to face the horse. Serafin lay on the straw, breathing heavily. *It's you or him*, he thought. *You. Or. Him.*

"Do it!" the kapo said, pressing his gun to Alexander's cheek. Alexander raised his arm, aimed the pistol at the horse's forehead and touched his finger to the trigger.

"I can't," he whispered, cursing his cowardice. "I can't do it."

The kapo snatched the gun from Alexander's hand. "Get out of my way." He shoved him aside and stood over the horse. "If anyone asks, I watched you do it." He fixed Alexander with a cold stare. "Now get out."

Alexander wandered the stalls and found himself

stopped at the entrance to the mare's stable. He slipped inside and grabbed a bucket. The mare's ears pricked up at the sound of a gunshot. Alexander heard it too. A single bullet spat into flesh.

Serafin was dead.

I'm better off without him, Alexander thought. He reached out to rub the foal's neck and found himself draped over the animal, his arms folded around the small body, his face pressed against the foal's neck. *No!* He shoved the foal aside and reached for the mare. *No going soft.* Soft could have got him killed just now. He wouldn't take that chance again. The only person – only thing – he had to take care of right now was himself. He forced his racing heart to slow as he pulled his cup from his belt and grabbed a teat to milk the mare. "He was a mean animal," he said, squeezing hard. "Mean and dangerous. Wouldn't have cared two hoots if the commander had put a bullet through *my* head." He sat back and dug his nails into his arm to concentrate his fury, sinking them into his freckled skin till it broke and he saw blood.

He felt the tears start. *No.* He leaped from the milking stool. *You will not cry for that horse*, he berated himself. *You'll go back to the stall and offer to help the kapo cart the body to the yard.*

He drained the milk from the bucket, wiped his face and stalked down the corridor, stopping at the open door to Isidor's stall. The boy's horse was crammed into a corner to make room for the swarm of men who stood in the room, haggling over a pile of sacks. Hessian sacks, stained red and bulging with … Alexander vomited on the straw. He'd seen men trade mice for cigarettes, seen them cook them over the open fire behind the stable. He'd heard of a Russian inmate who had shot a dog and sold the parts, but never a horse. Not a horse. Alexander ran from the stall.

"Alex, wait!" Isidor chased after him, pinning him to the wall. "They dragged the bags to my stall. They asked if I'd sell the…" Isidor's cheeks reddened. His hands slipped from Alexander's shoulders. "They asked if I'd sell the meat for them. I said no."

Alexander's knees buckled and he slumped to the floor. Isidor sat next to him, his arms looped around his legs. The sun dropped in the sky and the stall grew dark.

"I'm sorry about Serafin." Isidor pulled a beet from his pocket and offered it to Alexander. "I didn't know you'd grown close."

"We hadn't." Alexander felt a burning ache under his ribs. "It's just that … he did nothing wrong."

He stared at his shoes. "She didn't have to die." Alexander closed his eyes and saw his sister step from the cattle train.

"She?" Isidor interrupted, but Alexander wasn't listening.

"She was innocent. She trusted them. She trusted *me*." Alexander buried his head between his knees.

"I thought Serafin was a stallion, a male?" Isidor's brow furrowed. "Who is 'she'?"

"Lili," he said, looking up. "My sister."

"You have a sister?"

"I *had* a sister." Alexander stood up and dusted himself off. "I had a horse to look after too. Seems I don't have that either." His face grew hard. "But you've got something, don't you?" He pressed a finger to Isidor's chest. "You seem to have done well out of all this. From what I saw back there, you'll make a tidy profit." He shoved Isidor in the chest. "I don't care if you sell the meat. I don't give a damn if you carved it up yourself." He grabbed Isidor's shirt and balled it in his fist. "Just get me my share."

The siren sounded and the kapo called for the men to line up for inspection. Alexander peeled his fingers from Isidor's shirt, wiped his nose on his sleeve and walked to the yard between the silent trees, their bare branches stabbing the sky.

The clouds blotted out the stars and a sweep of cool air hit his face, but Alexander wasn't thinking about the coming winter and whether he'd survive the cold. He was thinking about tomorrow and whether he still had a job.

The Horse Platoon passed the checkpoint and headed back to their barrack.

The Rat's mean voice drowned out the sound of birds calling to each other. "*Hüpfen, rollen, laufen, drehen!* Drop and roll!"

A group of inmates dropped to their knees and rolled over on the gravel, their knees dripping blood onto their shredded trousers. Alexander looked up at the white stars. There was no God up there. The stories he'd been taught at Hebrew school were all lies. There was no reward for the righteous, no punishment for the wicked. He took a heel of bread from his secret pocket and handed it to the Rat. The man nodded his approval and stepped aside to let him pass.

Alexander climbed onto his bunk and pulled his blanket over his head. Isidor climbed up beside him, shoved something under the blanket and turned away. Alexander wrapped his hands around the offering: a mountain of cigarettes, tied with string.

"Your share," said Isidor, his voice wintry. "We're done."

Alexander slipped the cigarettes under his mattress, burrowed into his bed and waited, but there was no lump in his throat, no heavy chest, no guilt to beat down, no misgivings. *You're a fortress*, he said to himself. *A brick wall. A rock.*

So why did he feel so empty?

He woke the next day to lashing rain. He stepped from the barrack and turned up his collar, holding it around his neck to keep the water out. The Rat cleared his throat and reeled off the numbers of the men in the Horse Platoon. Serafin was dead and the commander was going to punish someone. Alexander held his breath. He was going to be sent back to Birkenau. The stablehands stepped forwards, one by one. The Rat looked up from his sheet of paper and called the last number: A10567. Alexander breathed out. He fell into line and followed the Rat to the square, his boots squelching as he pulled them from the mud.

The kapo was waiting for the Horse Platoon by the main gate, his face hidden under the canopy of a large black umbrella. Alexander had hoped to discover his fate from the kapo's expression, but he couldn't see the man's eyes so he waited to be called, his stomach in knots.

"A10567!"

Alexander shuffled forwards. He should've been glad his number was called. They wouldn't march him all the way to the stables just to tell him he didn't have a job. He should feel invincible. Instead he just felt tired.

The ground was soggy and Alexander's boots were spattered with mud and his pants wet by the time he reached the stable. The commander stood under the weeping sky waiting for his platoon, an officer beside him, holding an umbrella over his head. He counted the men and sent them to their horses except for Alexander, who was ordered to wait outside Chestnut's stall.

"I no longer require you to look after Chestnut. I've called for a new boy. Show him where Chestnut's equipment is kept and how to fix his feed," the commander said.

So, Alexander thought, this is it. My last day at the stable. Alexander walked to Chestnut's stall and slumped against the closed door. He heard Chestnut whinny inside and wondered whether he'd get to say goodbye to the pony, or reach into his bucket and steal one last handful of grain.

"Commander Ziegler wants Jacob to look after Chestnut," the kapo mumbled as he peeled off his dripping coat. "You'll work with him today, show him what to do and tomorrow he'll work on his own." He pulled a damp scarf from his neck and flung it over the stall door to dry. "Show him how to tack Chestnut up and which saddle to use," he said, yawning. Alexander searched the kapo's face for an apology, but his eyes were empty, his expression vacant.

"So I don't have a horse?" Alexander said.

The kapo's eyes brightened and a smile split his face. "Oh, you have a horse all right." He motioned Alexander towards Serafin's stall.

Alexander leaped back as the door swung open and two men lurched out.

"Bloody lunatic," the first man cursed, spitting a bloodied tooth into his cupped palm.

The second man limped out, wild-eyed and sweating. "Took us two hours to get him in there." He dragged one leg stiffly behind him. "Good luck getting him out."

Alexander backed away from the door as the timber bowed and snapped, the creature inside landing one explosive kick after another, until Alexander was sure the door would fly off its hinges.

"A10567," the kapo said, shoving Alexander towards the door. "Meet the commander's new mount."

Chapter 13

Alexander peered over the stable door and locked eyes with the commander's new stallion. The horse was backed into the shadows, his head tilted up to glare at Alexander, daring him to enter.

"What's his name?" Alexander gulped, lifting the cold metal from the latch. The horse's eyes widened and rolled back in his head.

"I don't know. The SS don't ask for names when they're seizing horses. The commander will see him next week. He'll name him then." The kapo peered through the door, looked at the horse and said, "If he's still here."

Alexander stared into the horse's soot-black eyes. So Ziegler only named his horses once he'd decided to keep them. Easier to dispose of them if they're not up to scratch. Harder to shoot them if they have a name. Just like *us*, Alexander thought.

The stallion raised his muzzle and bared his

teeth. He was coal-black save for a blaze of white on his muzzle and four perfect white socks. A big horse, maybe fifteen hands high, heavily muscled with giant, wide-set eyes and a broad forehead. An Arabian. Alexander pushed the door open and the horse charged at him, nostrils flaring, forcing Alexander to scramble out. He slammed the door behind him and rammed the latch shut just as the stallion smashed into the wood, bowing it and catapulting Alexander backwards onto the ground.

"Has the commander *seen* this horse?" Alexander stood up, panting.

The kapo nodded. "He likes his horses fiery."

The horse snorted and lashed out at the door, striking it with his hooves till the wood splintered and the walls shook.

Alexander respected a horse with spirit, but this horse wasn't strong-willed.

"He's not strong-willed," Alexander said. "He's deranged."

"Then sort him out." The kapo kicked the door and the horse shrieked. "The commander was embarrassed by Serafin. He doesn't want to have to dispose of another horse. He wants this one saddled and ready to ride Wednesday week. You have twelve days to break him."

This horse will do more than embarrass the commander, Alexander thought, feeling panicked. He'll throw him from his back, and when he does – Alexander's breath caught – there will be two bullets discharged that day.

"You can train the horse outside in the ring once the children have left and Chestnut's been put away." The kapo's face softened. "You'll do fine. He just needs a bit of gentle persuasion." He lifted the latch. "You've got a lot of work to do. Best get started right away." He swung the door open, shoved Alexander inside and closed the door behind him.

The horse's ears were flattened and his teeth bared. *See the pinned ears? He's going to lash out.* He heard his father say. *And the bared teeth? That means he's angry and wants to bite.* Alexander inched backwards until there was nowhere left to go.

"Easy, boy," he whispered, the blood banging in his ears. "I'm just going to wait here, till you calm down. I'm not going to move."

The horse gnashed his teeth. Alexander stared into his hard eyes, black as polished stone. He'd never broken in a horse. Sari was already wearing a saddle when he climbed onto her back and Paprika was too young to be ridden.

Alexander moved tentatively towards the horse

and extended his hand. The horse lunged and reared, striking at him with his massive hooves. When Alexander raised his arm above his head to protect himself, the horse's eyes flew open even wider. He kicked out wildly and Alexander had to flatten himself against the stall door to avoid being crushed.

"Good to see you're showing him who's boss." The kapo peered over the stall door as the horse plunged his feet back into the dust. Alexander gave him a vacant smile. He had seen men boss horses around, seen horses bound with rope, horses ridden blindfolded until they were too exhausted to buck. Horses tripped and tied down, horses beaten with belts until they were broken. When Paprika turned two, Alexander's mother arranged for Mr Gelbert to break her in. Alexander had stood at Gelbert's fence watching him saddle another boy's colt while he waited to usher Paprika into the ring. By the time the colt was returned to the boy, his hind legs were covered in blood.

Alexander stared at the Arabian. The hair on his neck had been rubbed away and the skin around the rope was worn thin. He stared at the noose hanging from the horse's neck and knew he wouldn't use it – couldn't use it – to subdue the animal. He wouldn't whip the horse into submission or tie him down.

The animal would only feel resentment and anger, the same anger he felt every morning when he woke in his plank bed and realized this wasn't all a bad dream. Bringing the horse to his knees would only instill fear in the animal. Alexander remembered the look of disappointment on his mother's face when he returned home from Gelbert's farm holding Paprika's saddle in his hand. He couldn't let Gelbert break the horse's spirit. He couldn't do it then and he couldn't do it now, especially here, especially in Auschwitz.

I'm not a rock. Alexander lifted his eyes to the horse's head. *All this time I've spent staring down the barrel of a gun and acting like no one else mattered, I wasn't getting stronger, I was whittling myself away.* Alexander slunk to his knees. He wasn't a brick wall. He was a shell, an empty husk, liable to blow away with the first gust of wind. He didn't know what tomorrow would bring and, for the first time in a long time, he didn't much care.

"I can't do this any more," he said, staring into the horse's dark eyes.

He stood up and walked towards the horse. Better to end his days in a stable at the wrong end of a horse, than die at the hands of an SS guard. He looked across at the stallion's muscled legs. *One swift kick to the head and it will all be over.* He took a step closer.

The stallion bared his teeth and spun around, lashing out with both hind feet. His kick missed its mark but knocked the shelf from the wall, bringing a bucket, a bottle of shampoo and a hoof pick tumbling down with it.

"What's going on?" Isidor swung the stall door open.

"Nothing," Alexander said, his eyes trained on the stallion. "I'm just getting acquainted with the commander's new mount."

"Getting acquainted or getting killed?" Isidor grabbed Alexander's sleeve and pulled him into the doorway, away from the animal. "You've lost your sister. But you must have someone else, someone who'll be waiting for you when this is all over..."

"I won't break him. I can't."

"So find another way," Isidor said. "You know horses better than they do."

Alexander lifted his eyes to the stallion's black face. There was only one way he was going to saddle the crazy animal and that was if the horse let him.

"I have a father and a mother," Alexander whispered, but Isidor had gone. He turned back to the stallion, careful not to lock eyes with the animal as he slunk back into the stall. He remembered how hesitant Paprika had been around him the first few weeks of her life. His father had told him that she saw him as a predator and that if he wanted to train her he had to gain her confidence, be her family. It had taken months for Paprika to trust him.

He had twelve days with the Arabian.

I have to be his family. Alexander lifted his gaze. The horse's eyes were narrowed, his mouth tight. Alexander took a deep breath and stepped closer. He heard the clack of teeth.

"I'm just taking a small step forwards. Very slow. I'm not going to touch you..." The Arabian's eyes flew open. He let out a piercing squeal and hammered the ground with his hooves. "Whoa!" Alexander looked up at the stallion. His flanks were dark with sweat, his body tense. "I don't want to be here any more than you do, but I have a job to do and if I don't do it, neither of us will make it out of here." The horse glared at him. "I won't hurt you. I promise." Alexander remembered his father's words. *A gentle word works better than a whip.* The Arabian lowered his head and stared at Alexander through his forelock.

Alexander bent down and scooped up a handful of hay.

"You hungry, boy?" He lifted his outstretched palm slowly. "Here, eat." The horse sniffed his palm and Alexander brought the hay to the stallion's lips, his fingertips brushing the horse's sweat-stained skin for just a moment before the horse jerked away. Alexander watched, frozen, as the Arabian reared up in fright before falling backwards into the dust, his muscled legs flailing, his eyes wide. Alexander knew that look. He'd seen it in animals and he'd seen it in men. He'd seen it in his mother's eyes the day his father was marched away, and he'd seen it on his own face the first time he saw his reflection in a mirror in Birkenau. The horse had the same look on his face Lili had when she stepped off the cattle train and saw the bald men in blue-and-white rags. The horse wasn't angry. He was scared.

"Someone must have hurt you badly," Alexander whispered. The horse clambered to his feet. "I couldn't save Lili." Alexander's knees shook. "And if the commander wants to dispose of you in twelve days' time, there's nothing I can do about that either." Alexander stepped away from the wall. "We've got twelve days. I can't promise we'll be here after that but I'll do the best I can."

He pulled himself up to his full height. The Arabian would feed off his mood. If he was anxious, the Arabian would stay anxious.

The Arabian. That wouldn't do. If he was going to train the horse, it needed a name. *Everyone deserves a*

160

name. Alexander remembered asking his father how Sari had got hers. *Your mother chose it,* his father had said, running a hand across the horse's arched neck. *Sari means noble lady. Perfect for her, isn't it?*

Alexander looked at the horse, his exposed teeth a white slash in his hard black face.

"Midnight," he said finally. "I'll call you Midnight."

Chapter 14

The horse stood in the shadows, panting. His legs were splayed, his head hung low to the ground. *Never waste the first few days of a foal's life*, Alexander remembered his father saying as he encouraged Paprika to take her first tentative steps away from Sari. *She's afraid, everything is new and she's looking to us to make this place home.*

Alexander lowered his eyes and let his head droop and his shoulders hang. His gaze seemed to threaten the horse, so maybe ignoring him would work. *I'll let him get used to my smell and my voice and then, when he trusts me, I'll strap a saddle onto his back and hand him over to the commander.* Alexander's heart pounded. *He's right to be terrified.*

The stall was cold but Alexander's hands were clammy. Midnight stood in the corner, his matted tail tucked between his legs. How do I let him know I don't mean him harm? Alexander's heart pounded.

If he wanted Midnight to be calm, he had to be calm. He slowed his breathing and tried to think of the last time he was relaxed, the last time he felt safe. He closed his eyes and returned to the kitchen at 6 Gregor Lane. His mother was making apple strudel, throwing the dough on the table and rolling it out, kneading and stretching it, adding slices of apple, raisins and cinnamon. The radio was on and his terrier, Spitz, was licking sugar from the floor. Alexander was eight and there were no yellow stars or barbed wire fences. He had a best friend and a place on the soccer team ... and then they took his father. Alexander swore under his breath. Every time he remembered, the memories turned black and made him want to crawl into a hole.

Midnight snorted and kicked out at the wall.

"What's going on?" The guard with the pock-marked skin called from the corridor. "Control your horse, or I'll whip the both of you."

"Yes, sir!" Alexander replied before the voice could come closer. "It won't happen again."

Won't happen again? Alexander raked his nails along his palms. You're an idiot, Altmann, an idiot without a plan. He unclenched his fists and shook out his arms. He had to stay calm. Maybe if he talked to the horse. He didn't feel like talking. He wasn't much of a talker at the best of times, but he had little choice.

"I can see why the commander chose you." He dropped his gaze and spoke in a low voice. "You're a fine horse. Straight fetlocks, no splints, long legs, good feet." Midnight unclenched his tail. The words seemed to soothe him.

The men who had dragged Midnight into the stall had left behind a carrot. Alexander scooped it from the straw and held out his hand. Midnight stomped his feet.

"It's for you," he hurried to assure the horse, careful to balance the carrot on his flattened palm.

"Take your time," Alexander said. He was trying to keep his hand still. Midnight turned and lunged.

"Owww!" Alexander yanked his arm from the horse's grip and stumbled backwards, swallowing his scream. His sleeve was torn and a length of bloodied cloth hung from Midnight's teeth. "You bastard!" he yelled, staring at his arm where the stallion's incisors had sunk into his skin. Alexander cradled his throbbing arm and clamboured to his feet. "Come any closer..." He grabbed a rake with his good hand and stabbed the air, fear and anger shunting away the pain. He lunged at the animal, a strange heat rising in his chest. His face grew hot and his throat tightened. "Think you can push me around? Think I'll just stand here and take it?" he hissed, aiming the prongs at Midnight. The horse backed himself into a corner and jammed his hocks against the wall. "Think you can do whatever you want and I won't fight back?" Midnight squealed and Alexander's skin prickled with heat. It felt good to fight back. Even if his anger *was* misdirected. He gave a final jab with the metal teeth and dropped the rake. He wasn't angry at the horse. He was angry at the world, angry at himself, angry with God.

He snatched the carrot from the floor, shoved it into his mouth and stared at the rope curled around the horse's quivering neck. It reminded him of a picture in a book he'd pulled from his father's bookshelf about the famous horse whisperer, John Rarey, who used to tie his horses' front legs up with rope. He'd force the animals to lie down so he could stroke them and show them they were safe. Alexander sighed. There was no way Midnight would let him near the rope and even if he could snatch it, he couldn't bring Midnight to his knees. He'd seen what the commander did to stablehands who tried to mount horses. He didn't want to think about what the man would do to a Jew who brought a horse to its knees. Alexander scooped up the rake and set it against the wall. He felt like he was in a deep, dark well with no way out.

A cold pain snaked through his arm and he shut his eyes and bent in half. There had to be another way.

Alexander rocked on his toes so his feet wouldn't fall asleep. His right leg was numb from standing frozen to the spot but he was still no closer to getting Midnight to trust him. He'd spent the last three hours ignoring the horse, trying to give the impression that they had plenty of time, that there was no reason to sweat, but the dark ovals under his arms gave him away. He had twelve days to saddle the Arabian, and no idea how to do it. Every time he took a step closer, Midnight snapped at the air.

His arm throbbed and his throat was dry. If only the horse could talk. If only he could tell Alexander what had happened to him to make him so skittish. The horse's head, neck and legs carried no bruises or scars. Neither his back nor his shoulders offered any clue as to what had poisoned him. Whatever damage had been done was more than skin deep.

"I get it," Alexander said quietly. "You've been treated badly. So have I."

Midnight snorted and pawed the ground.

"We've all seen our share of cruelty." Alexander

tried to find the right words. "You can't let it turn you sour." He lifted his eyes to the horse's flanks. "You can't distrust everyone you meet."

Alexander snuck from the stall to fetch the horse some water. The sky was grim, the clouds low and mean. He pulled his shirt close and hurried to the trough.

"What happened to your arm?" Isidor pulled his bucket from the water when he saw Alexander.

"Nothing. It's just a scratch."

"Just a scratch?" Isidor frowned. "Looks more like a bite."

Alexander lifted his bucket from the trough. He knew he should thank Isidor for slipping into his stall, for talking him around, for talking to him at all, but the words wouldn't come.

"It's the horse, isn't it?" Isidor hurried to the stable after Alexander. "If you need help—"

"I don't." Alexander turned his back on Isidor. "I'll be fine."

"I know." Isidor swung the stall door open for Alexander. "Still, the offer's there. If you need anything or if you want to talk," he reddened, "about the horse ... or your sister."

"No thanks," Alexander said, busying himself with the brushes. Talking about Lili wouldn't bring her back and whining about Midnight wouldn't tame him. He stepped into the stall and kicked the door closed behind him.

The horse drank greedily and, when Alexander set a bucket of warm mash down for him an hour later, he licked it clean. Alexander didn't try to wash the dried blood from Midnight's neck or brush the dirt from his hocks. He stood, eyes downcast, head bent, unmoving, hoping the horse would come to see him as part of the stall, no more threatening than the wooden door or the shelf. Alexander left the stall just three times that day, once for the water, once for the mash and once for the toilet.

He was dizzy with hunger by the time he slipped from the stall to join the platoon for the long walk back to Auschwitz. It was drizzling and his neck was itchy from his damp collar, the men smelled like wet sheep and his arm throbbed.

"Three dead." The kapo nodded to Hoess as they cleared the checkpoint. Alexander followed the kapo through the gates of Auschwitz, past the leafless birch trees and into the large brick building where once a month the platoon was shaved and disinfected. He left his rain-wet clothes on the bench and stepped into line, his right hand masking the gashed skin on his left arm.

He walked back to the barrack, dripping after his shower, his scalp stinging where it had been nicked, his arm throbbing.

"You want some?" A raw-boned Russian held out a square of stale bread. Alexander shook his head. He'd traded the cigarettes Isidor had given him for a scarf and had none left to trade. He climbed onto his bunk and pulled his blanket close but the cold found its way under his skin. Autumn would soon give way to winter and he had to be prepared, had to stockpile cigarettes and steal sugar cubes so he could buy a coat. He wondered whether Bauman sold hats. He'd need a pair of heavier pants too and thicker socks. *If I make it to winter*, he thought bitterly. *Eleven days. I have eleven days to break in a horse who's scared of his own shadow. Eleven days to put into action everything Father has taught me.* He breathed out, trying to loosen his panic. *I can't do it. I can't.* He dug his nails into his palm. *I don't know the first thing about taming a wild horse. Midnight knows it. And in eleven days, Commander Ziegler will know it too.*

Chapter 15

Alexander spent the next three days standing still as a post, waiting for Midnight to meet him halfway, to give him a sign or make the first move, but the plan wasn't working. His voice and his scent were as familiar to the horse as the wooden beams that held up the walls, but if he came within spitting distance, Midnight kicked out at him. He didn't trust Alexander any more than Alexander trusted the guards. The weather didn't help. The sheeting rain pounded the tin roof, setting the stallion on edge, and every time the sky rattled with thunder Midnight stamped his feet.

"So, I see he's still the boss." The kapo thrust his head over the stall door. "You have eight days." He nodded at Alexander and moved to the next stall. Alexander stared after him, angry that the kapo had seen what Alexander couldn't. *Of course we're not getting anywhere.* Alexander stared at the horse. *He's* still the boss! All this time he'd been trying to win Midnight's trust, when what he should have been doing was gaining his respect. When his father had told him that Paprika was frightened and trusting Alexander to make her a home, he'd said something else, something Alexander hadn't remembered until now. *She's looking for a leader to make sense of things.*

He peered down at his ragged clothes, his boots coming away at the heel and his stick-thin legs.

"I'm not much of a leader," he said, stepping away from the wall, "but I'm all you've got." Midnight's eyes grew round and he took a step backwards. "I don't know what happened to make you so skittish," Alexander continued, looking up into Midnight's black face. "And you know what? It doesn't matter. You're just going to have to trust me."

A bolt of lightning turned the sky metallic and Midnight leaped sideways. Alexander picked up a bucket and dipped his face into the water to drink it. He pulled a clutch of beets from the feed bucket and spooned them into his mouth.

"From now on, I eat and drink first," he said, planting the bucket on the ground and steeling himself. This was the closest he'd been to Midnight since the horse had bitten his arm. He didn't like to be crowded and Alexander had given the horse his space, when what he should have been doing was taking it from him. He scooped some beets into his hand and, avoiding Midnight's glare, walked towards the horse, pretending to look at something over his withers. He talked as he walked, cupping the beets in his hand, pretending to be brave as Midnight loomed larger. He could smell the Arabian's sweat mingling with his own. And then his right hand was under the horse's muzzle before Midnight had time to startle.

Alexander swallowed and steadied his hand, testing his will against the horse's. Close up, Midnight was even more daunting, his ink-black coat rippling over packed muscle, his neck backlit by the shards of white lightning. Alexander took a step closer and stopped shoulder to shoulder with the Arabian as the thunder relented and the rain turned to hail. It pounded the tin roof like bullets and Midnight squealed and fixed his eyes on Alexander, and then as if he actually believed Alexander to be the stronger beast, lowered his trembling head and blew through his lips. Alexander's mouth fell open. *He's letting me take control!* He lifted his flattened palm to the horse's lips and, not wanting to waste a moment, placed his free hand on the animal, letting it flutter there lightly, until Midnight stopped shuddering.

When Midnight had eaten the last of the beets and his belly was full and his eyes heavy, Alexander pulled his fingers from the horse's lips and picked up a brush. He'd chosen the softest brush on the shelf but standing there, with Midnight pawing the ground in front of him, he wondered if perhaps he was moving too fast. He held out his hand and waited, and within a few minutes Midnight was sniffing at the soft bristles.

Alexander lowered the brush to the horse's leg and Midnight started back, as if Alexander meant to hit him. He shushed him softly and swept the brush lightly over the horse's back leg in long, lazy circles until his tail unclenched and he stopped trembling.

"We need to clean you up." Alexander reached for a rag. The rope around Midnight's neck had scorched his skin and burned off his hair. Alexander dipped the rag into a bucket and brought the dripping cloth to Midnight's neck to wash the dried blood that had stiffened there, but when he squeezed the rag over Midnight's head, the horse's eyes flew open and when he went to drag the cloth over his poll and down between his eyes, Midnight leaned back and reared, his mouth wide as a cave and his massive forelegs sawing the air. Alexander leaped sideways as the horse plunged back to earth.

"OK," he panted, trying to slow his breathing. "I won't touch your head." He dropped the washrag into the bucket and cursed his luck. How the hell would he get a halter onto a head-shy horse? *With time*, his father would have said. *Time and patience.* But he didn't have time; he had eight days. He had to get the halter on Midnight today. Alexander ran through all the things he'd have to teach the horse before the Commander could ride him. His stomach grumbled, but he had no time for lunch. He bent down and shovelled a handful of hay into his mouth. It was dry and tasteless and scratched his throat, but he didn't spit it out. He chewed it until his saliva softened it to a pulp, then he swallowed it. You can get used to anything with time, he thought, dragging his hands through the straw. He'd got used to plenty in Auschwitz: blood, hunger, dirty smoke, death. He barely registered the sound of gunfire now. He'd heard it so many times, he'd become numb to it.

Alexander stared at Midnight and then looked across at the leather halter, hanging from its hook on the wall. "See something enough times and you lose your fear of it," he said. Alexander spun around and grabbed Serafin's halter.

"It won't hurt you." He grabbed the halter, held

it out and ran his fingers up and down the leather strands. "It's harmless," he continued, tossing it from one hand to another. Midnight lifted his dark eyes to watch. Alexander picked up the halter and balanced it on his head. He poked his finger through the brass rings and waited for Midnight to grow curious. Then he placed it on the ground and walked back and forth between the halter and the horse until Midnight's muscles relaxed and his spine loosened.

"OK. This time," he said, slipping the crownpiece over his neck, "I'm going to bring it with me." Alexander walked slowly towards the horse, stopping and turning on his heel as soon as Midnight moved away. The fourth time he approached with the halter, Midnight stayed still.

"Take as long as you need." Alexander held the halter out in front of him. "But not too long."

Midnight raised his head, took a step forwards and sniffed the leather.

"Good boy!" Alexander's panic melted away and he rushed to pat Midnight. He wrapped his arms around the horse's withers and pressed his cheek against Midnight's neck. "I told you we'd do this," he said, scratching him on the shoulder. It was Sari's favourite spot: the back of her shoulders where her neck met her withers. Alexander straightened and dropped his hands to his sides. He could feel himself slipping. *You're here to do a job*, he reminded himself. *Herd leaders aren't clingy. They don't try to make friends. They demand respect and reward good behaviour.* He took a carrot from his pocket and fed it to the horse, then squared his shoulders and turned his back on him.

Back and forth he walked, until his arms were aching and his back was sore. Up and down the stall until Midnight trusted him enough to let him touch the halter to his skin. When he accepted the contact without clenching his tail, Alexander took another carrot from his pocket. If the horse shifted his weight or tensed, Alexander walked away. He didn't need to punish the stallion for being afraid. Walking away from him was punishment enough. Midnight wasn't an angry horse. He was frightened and made more so when he was shunned and left alone. He was a herd animal; he was a horse. It was in his nature to seek out company.

The morning slunk away. Lunchtime came and went. It took Alexander three hours and a bunch of carrots to lift the halter to Midnight's nose without the horse turning away. He had to get Midnight outside soon. But if he rushed, Midnight would spook and he'd be back at square one. Over and over, he lifted the halter to Midnight's nose. Finally, in the late afternoon, with only a few hours of daylight left, Midnight dipped his head and let Alexander slip the halter over his muzzle. Alexander grabbed a handful of mane and pulled Midnight towards him, a smile splintering his face.

"Want to go for a walk?" He threaded the rope through the halter's buckle and headed through the door. He wished his father was here to see him halter his first horse. He brought his face up to Midnight's ear. "You'd like him," he said softly.

Three guards watched him lead Midnight from the stall. Let them stare, Alexander thought. Let them stare at the boy who tamed the wild horse. He marched past them with his chest puffed out and his head held high. Today he wasn't just another number: he was a herd leader, a horse trainer, a cowboy, a man. The kapo pressed a jumble of sugar cubes into his hand. Alexander slipped them into his pocket, tightened his grip on the lead rope and stepped into the yard.

The ring was empty and the yard deserted, save for two guards standing under a shelter of trees. Alexander opened his mouth and stuck his tongue out to catch the rain, glad to have traded a mound of cigarettes for a warm winter coat. It was good to be outside, even with the rain falling like a thick curtain and the ground a smear of mud. He'd been confined to the stall for days but this was where he belonged: in a ring, with a horse, his pockets bulging with sugar cubes, his clothes smelling of straw. Alexander's face flushed. Is this what it felt like to be happy? He couldn't quite remember. He stopped at the gate, his hand on the latch. He hoped it wasn't too soon to bring Midnight into the ring. The horse had been shut into his stall for four days, and before that, he'd been dragged through the yard, squealing.

A bolt of lightning tore through the sky. Alexander turned back to Midnight, horrified to see his ears pinned back and his nostrils flaring. He was wound tight as a rubber band. Alexander froze. He knew that look. It was the look of a horse about to bolt. He squared his shoulders and put on his meanest face. I have to be big – big enough to show him who's in charge. He jerked Midnight's head towards the ring, lifted the latch and kicked the gate open.

"Get in," he shouted, tugging at the rope, one eye on Midnight, another on the guards. Midnight snorted and the guards stopped talking.

"Come on, boy," Alexander begged, digging his heels into the mud. He tightened his grip on the rope. Midnight's coat was dark with sweat, his eyes wild.

"Control him!" one of the guards yelled, stepping from under the tree's canopy.

Alexander yanked on the rope but it was no use. The horse was three times his size and if he wanted to wrench the lead from Alexander's hand and rip through the yard, there was nothing he could do to stop him. Alexander panicked, as the rope slipped through his fingers.

"The lightning won't hurt you. Midnight, please," he whispered, as the guards ran towards him.

"You deaf?" the taller guard hissed. "Stop your horse misbehaving, or I'll stop him for you."

A bolt of lightning pierced the clouds. Midnight shrieked and leaped backwards, wrenching the lead from Alexander's hand.

"I'll stop him!" he heard one of the guards yell.

And as Midnight's legs thudded back to earth, Alexander saw the guard unbutton his coat and reach for his gun.

Chapter 16

Alexander looked up from his rope-burned fingers to see Midnight take off through the yard.

"Don't shoot!" he shouted at the guards as he sped after Midnight. A second streak of lightning turned the clouds silver and Alexander reached for the rope as Midnight stopped to lift his head to the sky. He caught its frayed end and dug his heels into the ground, but Midnight took off again, dragging him like a sack of grain across the rock-studded earth.

Alexander bounced along the rutted ground, hurtling towards the barbed wire fence, the earth tearing at his pants and ripping the buttons from his shirt. His palms were bleeding but he held on, sure that Midnight would stop, or at least slow, as they closed in on the fence. But instead he picked up speed.

Midnight galloped past the guards, flecks of foam at his mouth.

"You won't make it!" Alexander wailed. "The fence is too high!" He heard the click of a loaded gun and knew he should distance himself from the horse, knew he should let the rope slip through his fingers, but he couldn't. It was *his* fault Midnight was caught in the storm and if the horse flung himself at the metal barbs and tore his chest open, that'd be his fault too. Midnight rocked back onto his hocks and lifted his head.

"No!" Alexander screamed as Midnight lengthened his stride. "*Stop-p-p-p!*" he shouted as the rope flew from his fingers and his head hit the ground. He scrambled to his feet and wiped the grit from his eyes as Midnight's hulking body slammed to a halt in front of the fence. The guards shoved their weapons back into their holsters. With a thumping heart Alexander hobbled across the muddy ground towards Midnight. The horse was trembling and his tail was clamped down but there was no blood on his coat. He hadn't been shot. He'd stopped of his own accord. He'd stopped, Alexander realized, because he'd told him to. *I stopped him.* His heart ballooned in his chest. *I saved him!*

Midnight backed away from the fence, dipped his head and licked his lips. The horse was alive. Drenched in sweat and shuddering, but unharmed, because of *him*. He'd saved a horse. He'd saved a life. He reached for Midnight's mud-soaked back and rubbed him the way he'd seen Sari nuzzle Paprika. He'd promised Midnight he'd protect him and he had.

"It's going to be OK," Alexander whispered as the guards disappeared behind their umbrellas.

And for the first time, in a long time, he actually believed it.

"OK, let's do what we came here to do." Alexander swung the gate open and Midnight followed him into the ring. "Let's start with the basics." He pulled a sugar cube from his pocket, hoping to seal Midnight's trust, but when he unfurled his hand, Midnight startled and launched left, orbiting the ring in frantic circles.

Alexander stood in the dripping rain, the cold drilling through him, black mud seeping into his boots. He should've taken the horse back into the stable when he had the chance, but there wasn't time for apologies – it was almost dusk – and he wasn't about to let Midnight undo all the hard work they'd done. *If you're going to run*, Alexander locked eyes with the horse, *you're going to run because I tell you to*. He pulled a length of worn rope from the fence and flicked it at the stallion's feet, forcing him into a lope.

"You want to run?" Alexander yelled into the wind. "Then run."

Midnight threw his head back and took off around the ring, trotting fast and choppy, his eyes trained on Alexander, his ears turned towards him.

Alexander drove him on, pitching the rope at the ground, forcing Midnight around and around until his flanks shone with sweat. He paid no mind to the inmates watching him while they watered their horses. When the lightning abated he dropped his eyes to Midnight's shoulders and allowed the horse to slow, hopeful that he could close the gap between them, but was disappointed when Midnight skittered away.

"Oh, no you don't!" He blocked the horse's path. "You'll go where I tell you!" He flicked the rope and sent Midnight in the opposite direction, pressing him into flight until the horse relented and cocked an ear in his direction.

"OK, you can stop." Alexander dropped the rope and Midnight peeled away from the fence. He cantered towards Alexander, but as soon as the boy locked eyes on him, he broke away. Over and over, Alexander pressed him into flight, hoping the horse was smart enough to understand what he was trying to tell him: hold still and you can rest. Run away and I'll make you work.

A rock glanced off Alexander's shoulder and he turned to see the kapo standing at the stable door with a raised fist.

"Bring him in," the kapo shouted, lowering his arm. "We leave in half an hour." He hurried the last of the prisoners into the stable.

Alexander returned his attention to the horse. He had to get Midnight back into the stable.

"No stopping till I tell you," he shouted, beating down his panic as the last of the horses were put away for the night. Alexander glanced at the guards. Their guns were hidden but they were watching him.

"You heard the kapo, bring him in!" a guard yelled, kicking the gate open.

Alexander stopped, hung his arms by his sides and waited for Midnight to slacken, praying that when he approached him this time, he wouldn't bolt. Midnight ducked his head and slowed, and when he didn't move away, Alexander took a step closer. He reached into his pocket but it was empty.

"Sorry, boy. I don't have anything for you." Midnight raised his eyes to Alexander's pale hands and touched his nose to the crescent-shaped scars on his palm, his breath hot on Alexander's skin. "But if you come inside," Alexander said, his hands trembling as he reached for the rope that hung from the horse's neck, "I'll make it up to you."

Alexander lifted the rope and stepped towards the fence. He could hear the horse's footfall behind him as if an invisible thread connected them. He trusts me! Alexander hung his hands by his sides so he wouldn't wrap them around the horse. He bit his lip so the guards wouldn't see him smile. He was soaked to the skin, his head throbbed and his fingers smarted. His body ached as if he'd been beaten and yet he felt exhilarated. Midnight trusted him.

"You're back? Good." The kapo hurried Alexander into the stable. "We march out in five minutes!" Alexander nodded and turned to Midnight. He blew into Midnight's nostrils and the horse lifted his shiny eyes to Alexander's face and snorted back.

"Tomorrow we'll try the saddle," he said, stepping into the stall and pulling a horse blanket from the shelf. "What's wrong, boy?" Alexander's gaze dropped to the horse's left leg, and the thin red line leaking blood onto his hoof. Midnight's eyes narrowed in pain. He took a step forwards with his right leg, then limped onto his left.

Chapter 17

Alexander stood under the frozen clouds, waiting for the dawn order to march out of Auschwitz. Seven days. He had seven days left to get a saddle onto the commander's horse. The cold needled his body, despite the cardigan he wore hidden under his striped coat. *A present*, Isidor had said, dropping it into his lap the previous night and waving away the cup of soup Alexander had offered in return. *For breaking in the horse.* Alexander hadn't argued with or thanked Isidor, just fastened the broken buttons and slipped his arms through the fraying sleeves. *I didn't break him in*, he'd said, climbing onto his bunk. *You don't break horses. You tame them.*

Alexander rubbed his hands together to warm them. Perhaps I did break Midnight, he began to worry, imagining a fractured bone under the leaking blood on Midnight's leg. He shook the thought from his head. A crack or a tear could take months to heal. He had seven days and no options. Even if he'd had time to check Midnight's wound, he wouldn't have told anyone about it. The only person with authority to call the vet was the commander, and Alexander couldn't risk another visit from the vet. Not after what had happened to Serafin. Still, he felt miserable about it. He'd promised to protect Midnight. He'd asked the horse to trust him. No herd leader would have left a member of its herd alone and injured.

"They're all yours," the Rat said, handing the Horse Platoon over to the kapo.

"March out!" the kapo yelled, brandishing his stick. Alexander turned to face Herr Hoess at the gate. The commandant was wearing a fur-lined hat and a scarf pulled up to his nose. Alexander passed the checkpoint, pulled his threadbare cap onto his head and turned to face the front. Up ahead, in the half-dark, he saw a corpse lying in the mud, and a man leap out of line to drag it from the road. Alexander ran after him and they fell upon the body together, Alexander grabbing the wrists and the man taking the legs. Neither looked at the boy's blue face as they wrestled his gloves from his fingers and his boots from his feet.

"First in, best dressed." The kapo winked as

Alexander slipped back into line in front of Isidor, his face reddening as he pulled the dead boy's gloves onto his frost-bitten fingers.

"He didn't need them any more," Alexander whispered, not sure why he needed to explain. "If I didn't take them, someone else would've."

"I know," Isidor said, but he didn't sound convinced.

The men resumed their wintry hike. The cold found its way under Alexander's skin, making his eyes water and his nose run. He was sore and drowsy with lack of sleep, but he hurried on, anxious to arrive at the stable and see Midnight. As the first snatches of sky appeared in the east, the platoon entered the yard. The kapo gave the order and an armed guard threw the stable doors open. Alexander readied himself to sprint to the stall.

"Get to work!" the kapo yelled, dispersing the men. "Not so fast." He grabbed Alexander by the collar and dragged him back into line. "You can attend to the commander's horse later. Right now..."

Alexander shook free of the kapo's grasp. "Look, whatever you want me to do, I'll do it. Just give me a minute in the stall," he stammered. "Please."

"Can't do that." The kapo pulled his stick from his belt. "The commander wants to see you."

Alexander shut his eyes. The commander must have found out about Midnight's injury.

"What does he want with me?" The kapo shrugged, but they both knew the answer. The commander was an angry man. There were days he would enter the stable just to beat someone up. It's my turn, Alexander thought, swallowing hard. I kept Midnight's injury a secret and I have to be punished.

The commander appeared in the yard. "A10567?"

"He's here," the kapo answered for Alexander. "He's the boy looking after your Arabian. He's been making good progress."

The commander waved the kapo aside and took a step towards Alexander.

"Get in the car."

A black Mercedes sedan rolled to a stop. The commander slid into the back seat and motioned for Alexander to sit beside him. "Where I can keep an eye on you," he said, a smile smeared across his face. "And if you try to escape," he peeled his jacket aside and rested a hand on his gun, "I'll kill you myself."

Alexander sat on the soft leather seat, sweating into his shirt. He'd promised his mother he'd make it back to the farm the day he'd found her at the fence dividing the women's camp from the men's. It had been his third day at Birkenau. They'd fed their fingers through the wire fence and held each other's hands. *Lili's gone*, she'd said, gripping his fingers tight. *Live, Alex. Live, for all of us.*

He could see the commander's hands, hands that had beaten a stablehand to death for stealing a potato. The commander had thick, stubby fingers. Alexander's were bony. He looked at his scrawny hands and his insect legs. Next to him the commander's legs seemed bloated, his thighs swollen.

Alexander turned to the window. They were passing through a town, winding their way through the narrow streets, past a school and a library, a town hall and a park. Alexander smelled baking bread. He heard a child laugh and saw a man in a raincoat stop to pat a dog. He saw an elderly couple sipping tea inside a restaurant. A restaurant… Alexander pressed his nose to the glass.

"Take your cap off!" the commander barked as a woman pushing a stroller hurried into a doorway. "You're frightening them."

Alexander pulled his striped cap onto his lap and when the driver stopped the car at a set of black wrought-iron gates, the commander pulled his own hat from his head and dragged his fingers through his hair. He straightened his tie, buttoned his coat and leaped from the car, wrapping his arms around a small girl in a fur-lined coat, waiting by the gate.

"Papa!" A second girl threw her mittened hands around him, her breath misting in front of her. "We've been waiting for you."

"And we're cold," they trilled in unison.

The commander bent down and scooped the girl in the fur-lined coat onto his back, grabbing the mittened fingers of the second child and spinning her around.

"We'd better get you inside then." He laughed, dropping his hat onto black curls.

He has children. The thought made Alexander sick. The girl in the fur-lined coat had butter-coloured hair and slate-grey eyes like her father. The girl with the black curls had dimples. Like Lili.

"*Geh Raus!* Out!" A guard pulled Alexander from the car and deposited him at the door of a double-storey brick house. "And take your shoes off."

Alexander peeled his father's boots from his blistered feet, laid them carefully on the front porch and followed the guard inside, through a white-tiled entrance and down a hall. He sunk his toes into the carpet and scanned the smooth, white walls. There were pegs sunk into the wall for hanging coats and keys, and a side table cluttered with mahogany frames: sunshine and smiles trapped behind glass.

"Keep moving!" the guard barked, pushing Alexander past four closed doors, and one that had been left open. It looked to Alexander like a sitting room, with thick drapes pooling to the floor, a leather armchair, a bookcase and a small table cluttered with crockery, things he'd once taken for granted that now seemed magical: a teapot, a patterned china cup, a silver sugar spoon, a napkin. Things he could trade. Things he could eat. He looked past a vase spilling over with yellow flowers to the small garden visible through the window, where rhubarb grew in raised beds and spiky-leaved parsnips shared a bed with flowering cabbages.

"Take him to the kitchen," the commander ordered as he swept past the guard on his way down the hall.

The kitchen? Alexander's eyes grew wide.

The commander laughed. "You Jews, always thinking about your stomachs. I didn't bring you here to eat. I brought you here to work. We're down a Jew."

"Papa!" his daughters squealed as they swept past Alexander and caught their father on the stairs. "We've set the table in the sitting room and Mama's made us hot chocolate. Please." They each took a gloved hand and dragged their father back down the stairs.

"OK, *lieblings*. One cup, then it's time for your nap."

"Who's that?" the girl with the black curls pointed a woollen finger at Alexander. He looked down and saw what she saw – a boy with dirt-streaked skin and a grubby striped jacket.

"No one," the commander said, taking her mittened hand in his and pushing past Alexander. "Now, where's that hot chocolate you promised me."

Alexander stepped into the kitchen, his crusty feet leaving footprints on the floor.

"Wait here. A kitchen hand will be with you shortly," the guard said, leaving Alexander alone in the room. Alexander waited for the guard's footsteps to fade before lifting his eyes from the floor. On the wooden table in front of him was a loaf of fresh bread still warm in its pan, a roll of softened butter and a jar of dark plum jam. Alexander felt faint.

"Are you all right?" A woman appeared at the door, holding a basket of peas. Alexander nodded and looked down at his feet. He could feel the woman watching him. From the corner of his eye he could see the hem of a skirt and calfskin heels.

He watched them move across the white linoleum and saw them stop at the sink. He heard a cupboard door swing open and the clink of a glass under running water.

"Have a drink," she said, forcing a glass into his hand. Her nails were painted and on her left ring finger she wore a gold wedding band. A wedding band. Alexander stiffened. The woman was Ziegler's wife.

Alexander drank slowly, watching her through the refracted glass, her smile deepening the lines around her eyes. Her hair was blacker than her daughter's, her eyes greener. Alexander drained the water and placed the glass on the table.

"Thank you," he said, his tongue slippery in his mouth.

"What's your name?" The commander's wife asked, sweeping a stray lock of hair from her eye.

"My name?" Alexander straightened. "A10567."

"No." She shook her head. "Your name." She stared at Alexander and when he didn't answer, she held out her hand and let it hover in the air between them. "I'm Anna Ziegler, Herr Ziegler's wife. And you are?"

Alexander blinked again.

"Alexander Altmann," he whispered, the name

spiky in his mouth. He held out his hand. "Alexander Altmann," he said again, just to hear the words, to taste them. The commander's wife took his hand. She didn't twist it behind his back or tie it to the table leg. She shook his hand and let it fall, as if shaking hands with a Jew was a perfectly reasonable thing to do.

"Herr Altmann." She smiled. "Would you like a cup of tea?"

Alexander's mouth fell open – the commander was in the next room! He forced himself to speak.

"The commander – your husband – sent me here to work."

"Yes, thank you," she said, turning to the kettle. "And how about a slice of cake?"

She made him sit down. On a chair. At the table. She placed a slice of poppy seed cake in front of him and a cup of warm tea.

"One sugar or two?"

Alexander held up two fingers. He wished he'd cleaned his nails. He looked from the table to the door and back to the table at the slab of cake sitting there, plump with sugar and eggs. He pictured Isidor with a knife in his hand chasing mice around the stable and his own dinner – a wrinkled husk of onion he'd saved for a week. His stomach growled.

"It's OK." She smiled, sliding the plate closer.

He tore at the cake, forgetting his spoon, and sipped his tea, the sugar crystals exploding on his tongue. He sucked and chewed and swallowed, brushing the remaining scraps from the table into his hand before standing up.

"There are a few jobs outside. Perhaps we'll start with chopping wood." It almost sounded like a question. "The logs are outside." The commander's wife walked to the door. "We usually require two baskets of kindling."

Alexander shook the poppy seed crumbs into his mouth and followed her out. He didn't see the wood pile at first, nor the neat rows of carrots planted beside the parsnips, just the thick column of black smoke rising beyond the high brick fence. He cursed and pressed his eyes shut. It had been a good day. A cake day. His stomach was full. He turned his back on the smoke to feel the sun on his back, to forget for just a little while longer. *Is that what she did every time her husband returned from work?* he wanted to ask. *Every time she wandered outside and breathed the smouldering air or saw a half-starved child in blue-and-white rags: closed her eyes and pretended?*

"We'll see you again, I hope," she said, turning for the door. Alexander lifted the axe from the ground.

He wanted to say thank you, wanted to ask why she'd fed him and what she knew, but he nodded instead and bent over the wood, his confusion spilling out of him and staining his cheeks.

Chapter 18

Alexander walked down the commander's long gravel drive with a gun at his back, returning to Auschwitz in the dead of night. The camp was asleep. Even the dogs were silent. He pulled the barrack door open and, with the help of the moon, felt his way to the bathroom, flicking on the light and closing the door so he wouldn't wake the Rat. His bruises from the previous day were purpling and his torn palms made worse by the splinters that had found their way under his skin. He plucked them out, one by one, slipped his clothes off and stepped into the shower. The hot water stung his skin but the heat felt good.

He hurried across the cold cement floor, pulled himself onto his bunk, and froze. There was something in his bed, under the blanket. Something small and slick and cold. He reached out with his right foot and nudged it with his toes. When it didn't move, he dived under the blanket and pulled it out, holding it up to the moon's light to better make out its shape.

"It's for the horse," Isidor said, stirring, "but you can use it too." Alexander wrapped his fingers around the small glass jar, pried open the metal lid and smelled the contents. Garlic. Garlic and – he touched his nose to the paste – mint. Garlic to clean the wound and mint to dull the pain. Alexander turned to Isidor.

"How'd you know about the injury?"

"I saw you get into the commander's car." Isidor propped himself up on an elbow. "I offered to feed your horse and when I saw his leg, well, it looked pretty deep so I went to get—"

"The vet?" Alexander's face darkened.

"No, of course not!" Isidor sounded offended. "I went to get some medicine. I know someone at the infirmary, a chemist from Prague. I've done him a few favours. He owes me."

"Thank you," Alexander said quietly into the dark. He knew Isidor deserved more, knew that he owed him a conversation, or at least the beginnings of one, but that would mean tearing down the wall he'd built between them and winding back the silences, and he didn't know how.

"No problem," Isidor mumbled, his voice thick with sleep.

Alexander tucked the jar into his cap and slid it under his blanket. His father had always said that difficult times brought out the best and worst in men. Since coming to Auschwitz he'd seen only the dark side, until that was what he'd come to expect. That's why today had been so unexpected: stumbling into the commander's kitchen and meeting his wife; having her sit him down in front of a fire and chase the cold from his bones; offering him tea with sugar and poppy seed cake to beat down his hunger. She had looked at him and seen, not a prisoner, but a boy in need of food. A boy who wanted his name back.

Alexander turned over. He'd told himself the commander's wife was a one-time thing, and because he couldn't explain it, he hadn't tried. But now Isidor had brought him medicine and he couldn't help but think that if there were two good people in this awful place, maybe there were more. Maybe there was goodness to be found in people as well as animals. Alexander closed his eyes, and for the first time in a long time, slept a deep, dreamless sleep, in spite of the cold.

He woke before the others. The barrack was still

silent, not the enforced night-time silence, a different quiet, without wind or rain or the small sounds of life – tree branches scraping glass, flapping wings – the sounds one took for granted until they were gone. Alexander pulled his cap on and climbed down from his bunk. Something had changed. He tiptoed to the door, pushed it open and blinked at the bright white. While the camp had slept it had snowed!

Someone stirred in the bunk closest to the door.

"Shut the door or I'll shut it on your head." A boot sailed across the room and landed with a thud at Alexander's feet. He closed the door and waited for the Rat to emerge from his room. If he'd woken at home to a metre of fresh snow, he wouldn't be waiting. His boots would be on and he'd be flying out the back door. He'd be strapping on his skis to race Spitz down the hill or be building an arsenal of snowballs to hurl at his sister. He wouldn't be inside watching the world turn white.

When he was finally allowed out, the snow had already been sullied by the guards' heavy boots. But beyond the main gate, on the forest path that led to the stables, the snow glittered in the cold blue light. Outside the camp the ground was white and soft. The Horse Platoon walked between the naked trees, their feet wet and their fingers numb.

Alexander trudged through the snow, trying to catch the falling flakes with his tongue. His bones felt brittle but he'd slept well, and hidden under his cap was a salve for his horse. He ran to the stall as soon as the kapo blew his whistle. Six days. He had six days left.

Midnight was backed into the shadows and when Alexander entered, he dipped his head and looked away. *He's still unsure of me*, Alexander thought, stopping by the door. *Of course he is. I abandoned him.* He lowered his eyes to Midnight's leg. The blood that had dripped from his wound had dried and turned black. Alexander took a deep breath and walked towards him. He didn't know when he'd started sensing what Midnight was feeling but he knew, as he stood beside him, that the horse longed for his herd.

"I'm sorry," he said and slowly lifted his hand. Midnight detached himself from the shadows and, nickering gently, bumped his nose at Alexander's elbow. After everything that had happened, the horse still wanted to trust him. "Thank you," Alexander whispered. He ran his hands over the Arabian's neck. "I'll try to do better; I'll try to keep you safe." He wished he could do more – be more – for the horse, but he was just a stablehand. Midnight's life was in the commander's hands.

He filled a bowl with water and ran a sponge over Midnight's leg to loosen the dirt, while the horse explored him with sniffs and nudges. He dabbed Isidor's ointment onto the wound between feeding him handfuls of sweet hay and brought the horse a bucket of hot mash as a reward for his patience.

"Do you think you can walk on it?" he asked, grabbing a handful of mane. Midnight stepped towards the door with his right foot, then limped onto his left.

"They mustn't see you limp," Alexander whispered, and he led Midnight away from the door. He placed a hand on Midnight's neck and felt the horse's slow, steady pulse, and his own pulse slow to match it.

"We'll have to stay inside until you stop hobbling, but that's no reason not to work," he said, slipping from the stall to fetch the commander's saddle. He returned and dropped it onto the straw and waited for Midnight to grow curious. The saddle was made of brown leather, the seat a soft suede of the same deep brown hue. An eagle and a swastika had been burned into its leather hide and the stirrups had been engraved with the date of manufacture: 1940. The year his father had disappeared.

"It won't hurt you," Alexander said, picking up

a stirrup and turning it over. Midnight dipped his head and his eyelids sagged.

"We'll just leave it on the straw until you get used to it," he said. His own eyelids began to grow heavy. He wished he were more like a horse, able to sleep standing up, only needing two or three hours of broken sleep a night to make it through the day. Alexander yawned and edged closer to the horse for warmth. He thought of his little sister and the time she'd gone missing and how he'd searched for her and finally found her in the henhouse, asleep in the straw. He yawned again. *I won't sleep*, he thought. *I'll just rest for a moment.* He leaned against Midnight and let his lids close and, lulled by the drumbeat of Midnight's heart and his warm breath on Alexander's cheek, he fell asleep.

"Ow! What was that for?" Alexander woke with a start and rubbed his neck. Midnight bumped him again and tilted his head at the door.

"Just a minute." He leaped to his feet and brushed the straw from his clothes. "Oh, it's you," he said, flushing as the door flew open.

"Thought I'd come and see how your horse was doing." Isidor smiled and raised his hand to pat Midnight.

"Don't touch his poll!" Alexander cried, swiping Isidor's hand away. "You can rub his neck and his nose, but don't touch the top of his head. He's head-shy."

Isidor buried his hands in his pockets and bent down to inspect Midnight's leg.

Alexander pulled a brush from the shelf and ran it over Midnight's back. *What's your angle?* he thought, eyeing Isidor suspiciously. "Why'd you do it? Why'd you get me the medicine?" he asked finally.

"Because I *can*," Isidor said. Alexander folded his arms over his chest and waited.

"It's what I do." Isidor shrugged. "I get people what they want." He grabbed a comb from the shelf and dragged it through Midnight's tail. "It's how I've kept this job. The kapo likes his vodka and the guards know I'll get them whatever they need."

"But why me?" Alexander asked. "Why *me*?" He thought of all the favours Isidor had done him: the cardigan he wore under his striped coat, the medicine for his stomach cramps, introducing him to Karpowski and Weisz. It was a long list.

"You're the only one who never asked for anything." Isidor lowered the comb. "The only one who doesn't pretend to be my friend because he wants something from me."

Neither boy spoke for a long time.

"When my father was killed it was up to me to feed my brother," Isidor said without blinking. "My mother couldn't look after us so I had to learn quickly."

He has a brother. Alexander had never thought to ask, never thought he might have his own story.

"Turns out I was pretty good at wheeling and dealing. I was going to start a business selling second-hand clothes as soon as Hitler was overthrown. I'd even picked out a name: *Good as new.*" Isidor laughed bitterly. "What an idiot."

Alexander put down his brush and walked over to where Isidor stood.

"Mine was going to be called *The Galloping Stallion*," he said.

"The what?"

"Nothing." Alexander was quiet for a moment. "Your business isn't stupid. Stupid is telling your mother that you're going to enlist." Alexander filled a bucket and took it over to Midnight and the boys stood side by side listening to the horse lap the water. "I thought I'd make a great soldier. Boasted that my horse would be the finest in the regiment. *God help the Germans if they have to fight the two of us!* I *actually* said that." He blushed. "I pictured myself in the uniform. I didn't picture *this*." He looked down at his wiry arms and spit-flecked pants.

"What? The two of us talking?" Isidor's face split into a smile. "I knew I'd break you eventually."

Chapter 19

Four days passed. The temperature dipped below freezing and the guards pulled the collars of their heavy winter coats around their beefy necks and buried their double chins under scarves, while the Horse Platoon trudged between the camp and the stables, their bodies wilted by the heavy snow. Alexander traded his cigarettes for a pair of woollen socks, but the cold found its way through the holes in his shoes to his toes and his feet. The only way he could warm himself was by clinging to Midnight. They stood cheek to cheek, waiting anxiously for the horse's leg to heal, Midnight's steaming breath on Alexander's frozen skin, warming him. And as the hours passed they began to thaw, and as the days passed a friendship grew. Alexander found his heart quickening every time he walked to the stall, knowing Midnight's ears would perk up at his approach, and he'd feel a rush of gratitude as he swung the door open and Midnight limped towards him, for here was someone who was happy to see him.

Isidor snuck into Alexander's stall to talk whenever the guards' backs were turned and Alexander let him. He didn't say much but he liked to listen – the sound of Isidor's voice filled his head and left no room for remembering. The noise beat back his guilt. He learned that Isidor's best friend's name was Erik and his most treasured possession was a three-speed bicycle – and that he'd lost them both on the same day when Erik turned up at the park with a gang of Hitler Youth and slammed Isidor's bike against a tree. *We're not that different*, Alexander thought. It didn't make him feel any better, but it made him feel a little less alone.

Outside the stable, thick snowflakes fell. The cold made the guards icy and the inmates irritable, but Alexander hid away in Midnight's stall and taught the commander's horse to come at his whistle and stop at his raised hand, always aware of time slipping away. He brushed the commander's saddle along Midnight's flanks and let the horse run his tongue over its leather stirrups. He slung it over his shoulder when he mucked out the stall and draped it beside the feed bucket to strip it of mystery and make it familiar. He made up buckets of hot mash to share between them and tended Midnight's sore leg until the wound closed and healed and he no longer limped. And then, with one day to go before Commander Ziegler came for his horse, Alexander crossed his fingers and slipped a saddle blanket onto Midnight's back. He smoothed it out and, when Midnight didn't spook, held his breath and lifted the saddle from its hook.

"Time's running out," he said, lowering it gently onto Midnight's back. He lifted the bridle over Midnight's ears, secured the reins and took the stirrups down. "The commander's coming for you tomorrow. Let's get you outside."

Midnight stood at the stable entrance, the cold dawn light reflected in his large, bright eyes. He took a step into the yard, lowered his head and sniffed the frozen ground, the snow flurrying around him, soft as icing sugar. He eyed the white powder and pawed it gently, surprised when it shifted under his weight. Alexander walked him around the yard, acquainting him with the other horses and getting him used to the deep cold and the bright white.

Midnight turned towards the stable and sniffed the air.

"What is it?" Alexander asked, peering through the fog. Two inmates stepped aside and Alexander saw one of the stablehands hanging from a hook that had been drilled into the stable wall. The boy's lips were frozen shut but his eyes were open. His pants hung around his ankles and an upturned milk bucket lay in the snow at his feet. Alexander felt queasy. He knew the boy. He didn't know his name but Alexander had snuck into his stall every day to milk his mare. *I showed him how to milk her so he couldn't turn me in. I told him to drink it.* Alexander looked at the battered tin bucket with the red handle that lay at the boy's feet, the same bucket they both used to milk the mare. *I told him it was safe.* Midnight followed him into the stall and he closed the door behind them, wondering whether he'd ever be able to paste new memories over the old ones. If he made it home, would he be able to work in his own stable? Or would a bucket mean dinner and a horsewhip twenty lashes?

"So, he's OK?" The kapo poked his head over the stall door. "The commander's horse is well?"

"Why wouldn't he be?" Alexander's jaw twitched.

"His leg..." The kapo's eyes tunnelled into Alexander's. "I wasn't sure..."

"He's fine."

"Good. The commander will be here tomorrow at eight." The kapo let the words sink in. "Have the horse saddled and ready to ride."

211

* * *

The stable was quiet. The men were at lunch and the guards gathered outside the lunch room keeping an eye on them. Alexander slid his left foot into the stirrup, not daring even to breath. *You've got no choice*, he told himself. *If you send Midnight out to the commander not knowing what it feels like to have someone on his back, he'll buck, and you'll both be shot.* But it wasn't just that. Alexander wanted to be the first person to climb onto Midnight's back. He'd tamed him and trained him and there was no way the commander was going take that away from him. They'd worked too hard.

He grabbed the saddle and hoisted himself up to stand in the stirrup, hovering there to let Midnight settle into the strangeness of it, letting him get used to his weight and seeing someone from above.

"I'm just going to lay across your back now. I'm not going to sit yet," Alexander whispered, his heart racing as he draped himself across the saddle, his legs hanging off one side of the horse, his head the other.

It felt good to have a horse under him, to feel its beating heart and smell its dusty odour. Alexander's skin prickled. He pulled a marble of ice from Midnight's mane and managed not to cry.

"Good boy," he cooed when Midnight stood his ground. He reached out to touch the velvet of the horse's muzzle, glad that Midnight welcomed his touch.

When both their hearts had stilled, he eased his right leg over the horse and hoisted himself up to sit in the saddle, dropping his chest onto the horse so he couldn't be seen over the stall door. He thought of Sari, waiting for him at the end of Gregor Lane, and he allowed himself to hope that he might survive the war. And that his parents might too.

"We'll make it through this," Alexander said, wrapping his fingers around the reins and tugging gently against Midnight's neck, knowing the commander would pull back harder and might even use the whip. "You do this for the commander tomorrow and we'll be just fine." He stroked Midnight's chiselled neck and closed his eyes. He pressed his feet into Midnight's flanks and imagined the two of them soaring, flying, free, Midnight's hooves flattening the ground, the clouds whipping past, the camp receding. Alexander dropped the reins and wrapped his arms around Midnight's belly. He knew he shouldn't cling to something he could so easily lose, but he was tired of running from his feelings, tired of beating them down. He pressed his cheek to Midnight's neck and felt something unlock inside him.

"Is he ready?" The door groaned on its hinges and Isidor slipped into the stall. "I heard about the commander—" His mouth fell open as he saw Alexander's feet hit the ground. "You weren't just—" He adjusted the stirrup swinging at Midnight's side.

"No," Alexander cut him off, his heart hammering in his chest. He walked to the back of the stall and picked up a bucket.

"Oh," Isidor said, sounding disappointed. He reached into his pocket, pulled out a potato and handed it to Alexander. "So is he ready?"

"I don't know." Alexander took the potato and bit into it hungrily. "He didn't buck me off." He attempted a smile. "But, tomorrow ..."

"... he'll be fine," Isidor finished his sentence. "You've trained him well. He knows what to do."

"He trusts me," Alexander said, slipping the feed bucket under Midnight's nose. "I don't want to let him down."

"You can't control what happens next."

"So if the commander pulls out his whip or his gun, I do nothing?" Alexander asked.

"What *can* you do?"

Midnight lowered his nose to the hay and ate,

214

while the boys stood either side of him, not talking.

"Well, good luck," Isidor said, turning for the door.

"My sister, Lili," Alexander spoke quickly, "was ten years old when she died." He hadn't meant to say anything, but there it was. It felt good to hear her name out loud, his silence had made her small. "And I did nothing," he continued. "I said nothing."

Isidor swung around to face him.

"We climbed out of the cattle train." Alexander's voice was low. "Lili was crying. She was scared of the guns and the dogs on chains." He shut his eyes and let his sorrow form words. "Of course she was scared. I was scared too, but I wasn't going to give them the satisfaction."

Isidor nodded.

"So, she was crying…" Alexander's shoulder's sagged. "And I told her to grow up. Told her to stop being such a baby. It only made her cry harder. And I was too mean to comfort her. She wouldn't talk to me after that. Not even when we were told to line up. Women and children on one side, men on the other. My mother told me to go with the men." His words tripped over one another as they tumbled out. "I didn't want to. I'd told my father I'd look after my sister, but Lili said no. 'I can look after myself,' she said." He let his words twist around the memory. "So I went. I walked off to the left and she went right. To the gas. We never got to say goodbye."

"You couldn't have known," Isidor whispered.

A whistle blew and footsteps filled the corridor.

"You better go," Alexander said, opening the door.

"My brother's name was Isaac." Isidor stood in the doorway, trying to find the right words to fit his pain. "He was twelve and a half. He loved soccer. He was a smart kid but he hated school, couldn't stand being told what to do. He would've hated it here." He gazed out the window at the white clouds. "Maybe they've met." He attempted a smile. "My brother, Isaac, and your sister, Lili."

Chapter 20

Alexander stepped into the yard clutching the lead rope, his legs shaking under his baggy pants. He hated that he had to hand Midnight over to the commander. It felt like a betrayal, even though Midnight wasn't his horse. And never would be.

"C'mon, boy," he whispered, nudging Midnight into a walk. He wanted to tell him that everything would be OK, but he couldn't get the words out. He couldn't lie to Midnight, not after all they'd been through.

He wished he'd prepared him better, but he didn't know how. How do you prepare a horse when you can't squeeze your knees against its sides and take off into the hills? Alexander's brow shimmered with sweat. The kapo was already outside handing the commander his riding crop. Midnight snorted and tossed his head, his panic rising to meet Alexander's.

Alexander exhaled. If he wanted to calm the

horse, he had to stop his own heart hammering. He wiped the frost from Midnight's flanks and pressed his body close to the horse's, making his breath as slow and even as he could. Midnight shifted uneasily and took a small step sideways.

"Please." Alexander pressed his cheek to Midnight's neck.

He walked towards the commander and Midnight followed, stopping in front of the commander when Alexander raised his hand. "Good boy." Alexander spoke softly, reaching over to pat the horse.

"That'll be all!" the commander said, warning Alexander away with his crop.

Midnight stiffened and took a step back. *It's OK*, Alexander thought, looking into the horse's dark eyes, willing him to understand. *Just let him up onto your back and we'll both be OK.*

He backed away from the horse. He could hardly bear to watch. The commander snatched the reins, pulled a black boot from the snow and slid it into a stirrup. Alexander thought about praying, but if he couldn't trust God to keep his little sister safe, what chance did he have with a horse? "Let him behave," Alexander begged the clouds, the sky and the trees instead. "Don't let him end up like Serafin." A knot formed in the back of his throat. He hadn't protected

Serafin. Nor had he grieved for him. *I should've been kinder*, Alexander thought.

Commander Ziegler sprung off his left foot, swung his leg over Midnight's broad back and settled into the saddle, his face relaxing into a smile. He couldn't see Midnight's nostrils flare as he landed on his back, but Alexander did. He saw the horse's eyes bug out and his ears twitch. It reminded him of his dog, Spitz, waiting for Alexander to throw him the ball when they played catch, his neck straining, his small body coiled tight as a spring.

"Be back here in two hours," the commander called to Alexander as he took up the reins and swung the horse towards the gate.

Two hours! Alexander closed the stall door and fell back against the hard wood. *Midnight had taken off at a trot without being asked, but would he take instruction? And what if the commander whipped him?* He grabbed a rake. Maybe if he mucked out the stall, the sound in his head would stop – the pounding of Midnight's hooves on the snow as he slid into a canter and disappeared into the fog.

Alexander changed the straw and prepared a tub of corn for Midnight's return. "He'll come back," he said to himself, "and he'll be tired and cold."

He pulled a blanket from the shelf and lugged it

outside, the snow swirling around him. It settled on his shoulders and slid down his neck. It turned his fingers blue and his breath white. The kapo hadn't sent him out to wait for the commander but he couldn't stay inside the suffocating stall a moment longer. He tucked his hands under his armpits and waited.

He heard Midnight before he saw him, the muffled thud of hooves on snow, the thumping three-beat gait, then a black smudge against the bright white and finally, Midnight, shiny-eyed and panting, his black coat glistening, his breath steaming in front of him.

The kapo joined Alexander as Midnight slowed to a stop.

"Now *that's* a horse!" the commander trumpeted, his face full of admiration. "Up to a gallop within seconds. Didn't even have to pull out the whip. I've called him Blitz. It seemed fitting." The commander slid off the horse and dropped the reins. "Have him ready tomorrow at two and shorten the stirrups. I'm going to take him jumping."

Alexander scooped up the reins, threw the blanket over Midnight's soaked back and returned him to the stall. *Blitz! The German word for lightning, the one thing that terrified Midnight and made him want to bolt.*

"He can call you whatever he wants," Alexander whispered into Midnight's ear, "but your name is Midnight." He looked down at the number etched into his skin. "And mine is Alexander," he said, realizing the horse might never have heard his name. "Alexander Altmann." He stared into the horse's dark eyes. *How am I supposed to teach you to jump when I can't climb onto your back? Either the commander is a fool, or he wants us to fail.*

Alexander lifted the blanket from Midnight's back. The horse was breathing hard but he was fine. He hadn't been whipped and – he ran his hands over the horse's back, belly and legs – Alexander didn't have any scratches or bumps. "You had me scared today," he said, touching his forehead to Midnight's muzzle. Midnight nickered and brought his face close to Alexander's, close enough to rub his pink sandpaper tongue across Alexander's cheek. Like a kiss. Alexander touched his fingers to his wet cheek and his throat closed over. He'd never known a horse to lick anything other than a salt block.

He scooped a fistful of straw from the floor. "Let's get you dry," he said, rubbing the wisps over Midnight's body. "Then we'll see about jumping." Alexander unfastened Midnight's noseband, slid the bridle off and took the bit from his mouth. He lifted the snow-dusted saddle from his back, picked up a bristle brush and rubbed the ice crusts from his legs and combed the knots from his tail.

"Want something to eat?" He dragged over a bucket of water and the tub of sweet corn.

Midnight bent over the tub and nudged it towards Alexander. "How odd!" Alexander stared at the tub. *That's not a trick I taught you.* Neither was the kiss. Alexander looked at Midnight as it dawned on him: someone else had taught Midnight to share his food. Someone who'd known him before he was a head-shy horse without a name. Of course someone had loved the Arabian before the war brought him to Auschwitz. Cared for him, taught him tricks, loved him, and then lost him. Alexander looked into Midnight's black eyes. Something bad must have happened to him on the way to Auschwitz. Something bad which had stripped away his trust and made him wary of people.

"You can jump, can't you?" Alexander asked, remembering the day lightning had struck in the yard and the way Midnight had flown at the barbed wire fence, lengthening his stride, then rocking back onto his hocks as he closed in on the jump. "The people you lived with before you came here taught you, didn't they?" He smiled and, forgetting that the horse was head-shy, stretched out his hand to sweep his fingertips over the white blaze between Midnight's eyes.

"Whoa!" Alexander flew backwards as the horse snorted and drew his head away sharply.

"I'm sorry! I forgot…" he stammered. "I won't do it again."

The Horse Platoon walked home in the dying light, past frozen paddocks and roads slick with ice. By the time Alexander returned to Auschwitz, the sky had darkened. The stars had no reason to sparkle and the sky was black, but inside the barrack a flickering light led the way to his bunk.

"Hanukkah!" Isidor's mouth curved into a smile at the sight of the Rat standing in the middle of the room clutching a candle. "It's the first night of Hanukkah." He stepped out of his wet boots and hurried to join the group of men huddled around the barrack boss.

"Baruch Atah Adonai Elohenu Melech Haolam," the Rat intoned.

"She asa nisim la-avotenu bayamim hahem bizman hazeh," the men joined his Hebrew prayer, hope flickering in their red-rimmed eyes. The Rat flinched

as the melting candle burned down to its wick, once again plunging the barrack into darkness.

"Blessed are You, Lord our God, King of the Universe, who performed miracles," he continued in the dark, repeating the Hanukkah story that Alexander's mother had told him when he was young. It had seemed wondrous then, Judah the Maccabee liberating the second temple from the Greeks and the miracle of the oil that burned for eight days.

"I don't believe in miracles," Alexander said to no one in particular. But that wasn't entirely true. He'd witnessed wondrous things as a child: eggs cracking open to reveal clammy chicks, a mare giving birth, a rainbow touching snow. And even here: a horse's kiss. They were all miracles, in a way. Miracles of nature even Hitler could not destroy.

Alexander fell asleep dreaming of shooting stars but woke to the sound of men being chased from their beds and the smell of unwashed bodies. Breakfast was a scrap of bread and a spoonful of snow. There was no time for coffee: the Horse Platoon was to march to the delousing block before sunrise.

"And the rest of you," the Rat turned on the other men, "clean this place up. It looks like a chicken coop. I want to be able to eat off the floor."

"But we were disinfected two weeks ago!" Isidor

complained as the Rat chased the Horse Platoon from the barrack.

Alexander stepped into the disinfecting hall, bowed his head and waited for the razor, then followed the other broken-down bodies into the scalding showers and then into the yard to drip-dry, knowing that as soon as he pulled his dirty jacket on, he'd be covered in lice again. But his jacket was gone and in the hall, on the bench, in its place, was a neatly folded pile of clothes, an untarnished metal bowl and a shiny round spoon. The jacket had all its buttons and the pants had no holes. Alexander frowned. It would take him weeks to save enough cigarettes to pay the tailor to sew him another secret pocket. Isidor held up a pair of socks and shrugged.

At lunchtime Alexander found a piece of meat in his soup and a few minutes after that the commander whisked a man with a clipboard through the stable. He wore a heavy grey coat with a red and white armband on his left sleeve.

"Red Cross," Isidor whispered.

The man pulled the ladle from the soup tureen and held it up to his nose.

"Beef," the commander offered. "Yesterday it was cabbage and beet. Would you like to see the stalls?"

The man nodded, scribbled something on his clipboard and followed the commander out. Alexander watched him walk through the stable as if it was a museum, taking pictures of the stablehands in their buttoned-up jackets, their skin shiny from the showers, their breath smelling of meat. The Red Cross man smiled at something the commander said, shook his hand and followed him into the yard. The kapo waited till they were gone, then carried away the soup.

Ask about the places left off the itinerary, Alexander wanted to shout. *Go to Birkenau and ask to see the crematoria. Ask about the gas.* But he kept his mouth shut. The guards had pulled out their guns again.

When the commander returned to the yard later that afternoon, Alexander was waiting for him, his fingers frozen around the lead rope. He handed the commander the reins and watched him take Midnight through the gate, the fog closing in on them as they sped up to a gallop.

"It should've been me on his back," Alexander said through gritted teeth, imagining the commander closing in on a jump and letting his weight sink to his heels as he tilted forwards and slid his gloved hands up Midnight's neck. *It should have been me taking him over that first jump.* Alexander unfurled his fists and slunk back to the stable.

The hours dragged by. Alexander polished the tack, oiled the hinges on the door, mucked out the stall, prepared Midnight's feed and returned to the yard. Out there in the leafless winter there was nothing to distract him from his gnawing belly, nothing to warm him but his memories. He shovelled a handful of snow into his mouth and gave in to them.

It was the previous winter. Alexander was thirteen and Lili was nine. A lifetime ago. Lili was in the yard standing next to the snowman he had built, with a carrot in her hand. *It's for his nose*, she'd said, tossing him the carrot. He'd plunged it into the snowman's face, above the small black moustache he'd fashioned from an old broom. *He looks like Hitler*, Lili had said, staring up at the snowman's raisin eyes. Alexander drove the broom handle into Hitler's side, tilting the arm up in a Nazi salute. *Ladies first*, he'd laughed, snapping a branch from a tree and handing it to Lili. Alexander smiled, remembering how she'd pounced on the snowman. She'd plunged a stick through his guts and another through his eye, yelping with delight. The snowman's arm broke, his nose fell off, and when his head rolled off and his body crumbled, they'd trampled him to the ground until he was nothing more than a dirty heap of snow.

Alexander shook the memories off as Midnight

came galloping through the gate. He was sure that the horse had taken the jumps easily, but he wanted to see – needed to see – the commander's ugly smile, just to be sure. Alexander shuddered at the sight of so many perfect white teeth. *There's no such thing as miracles*, he said to himself. All he could hope for was days like these: meat days, days when he was left alone to dream. Days which ended with his fingers around a lead rope and his cheek pressed against Midnight's neck.

On the eighth day of Hanukkah, as the men were marching to the stable, the sky lit up with fireworks. The snow-laden branches of the trees glowed orange and the frozen ground shimmered in the early dawn. The guards lowered their guns and looked up at the exploding sky.

"Monowitz is burning!" Isidor shouted, a smile stretched across his pink face. Alexander pulled his hands from his ears. He'd heard of Monowitz, another in the long list of work camps scattered around Auschwitz. Men who were sent to Monowitz to work in the mines lasted less than a month. Those who got jobs in the nearby Farben chemical plant lasted longer. Alexander searched the sky for planes. He'd heard the stablehands talk about the Allies coming to save them. He didn't pay them any attention. Their talk of advancing Soviet troops made them feel better, but that's all it was – desperate talk. He chose not to listen, chose to ignore the rumbling planes too. He'd heard the bombers months ago – it was before Jewish New Year and he'd hoped the rattling sky heralded a new beginning. But it had changed nothing. The Rat still pulled them from their beds each morning, the kapo still marched them to the stable, the commander still beat them.

As soon as the Horse Platoon arrived at the yard, Alexander charged at the stable door. He could hear the sound of hooves crashing against wood and Midnight's high-pitched whinny. He flung open the stable door and ran to Midnight's stall, past a grey mare trying to escape her stall, and a bay stallion hurtling for the exit. He threw open the door to see Midnight backed against a wall, his feet splayed, his ears pricked, trying to make sense of the blasts. He was panting in short, nervous snorts and his body was trembling. He was terrified.

"It's OK." Alexander let his hand hover in the space between them. Midnight had been wrenched from his home, he didn't like surprises. He needed familiarity: a smell he recognized, a voice he trusted, a friend. Midnight lowered his nose and snuffled Alexander's fingers and when his breathing slowed, Alexander hushed him gently and placed his hand on Midnight's neck until the horse's body grew still.

When the stable shook a second time and the sky glowed orange, Midnight's eyes widened but instead of starting back he nickered and put his face forwards for Alexander to rub. With his heart churning, Alexander pulled his hand from the horse's neck and swept his trembling fingers along Midnight's wet nose, and when the horse didn't move, trailed his hand up Midnight's soft white blaze to his forehead. *I'm touching his head.* Alexander held his breath. *The top of his head!* He swept his fingers over the soft skin of Midnight's poll and rubbed him between his black eyes, tears sliding down his cheeks. It felt good to feel something other than guilt, to have pride butt up against regret and joy trump shame. To feel like he mattered. To feel whole. To feel hope.

"They're coming to save us," he whispered in the crackling silence between bombs.

Chapter 21

The days folded into each other and soon it was Christmas. Birkenau's blackened chimneys had stopped spewing smoke and the Allies' bombs rained down on Monowitz. The distant rumble of gunfire made Alexander's heart balloon in his chest. He stood, half-starved, next to his well-fed horse, looked up at the beautiful, frightening sky and dared to imagine stepping beyond the barbed wire without a gun at his back. He pictured himself walking down Gregor Lane and opening his front door.

At night he closed his eyes and the Rat's footsteps became his father's, the whispers from surrounding bunks, his mother's quiet voice. "The Russians are coming," he whispered to the walls and the floor. "They're on their way!"

It was so close to the end of the war – and so close to getting home – he could *taste* freedom. *It's just a matter of time*, he told himself. *I have no choice but to survive.*

231

He tore the mould from his bread and cut what was left into thin slices so it would last. He swapped his cigarettes for an extra pair of socks and let Isidor fall asleep butted up against him so they could keep each other warm.

Alexander tried his best to avoid the guards, who'd grown sombre and taken to drinking, and the commander, who'd grown angrier and more violent with each day. He no longer beat the stablehands he caught smuggling food from the stables – he shot them. He didn't hurt Midnight, but he rode him fast and hard. He seemed to be chasing something. "Whatever it is," he told Isidor, "he won't find it on the back of a horse, no matter how hard he rides him."

While the commander's mood worsened, the Rat, sensing the end of the war was near, sought to switch sides. He stopped taking the men's food and only beat them occasionally. On New Year's Eve he got his hands on a few extra loaves of bread and divided them among the men, tossing the last piece onto the floor so the inmates could scrabble over it.

"Happy New Year!" He stumbled towards Alexander and held out a bottle. Alexander wrapped his lips around the mouth of the vodka bottle and pretended to take a swig. He wasn't going to share his first drink with the Rat. He'd drink to the death of the German Reich. He'd drink to his first night back home. He'd drink with his father to celebrate a new beginning, but he wouldn't drink to blur the hard edges of the barrack or the Rat's mean smile. He didn't want to forget, not when he was so close to the end, so close to going home. He owed it to Lili, and to himself, to remember everything the SS had done to them.

He took note of everything – the bodies stacked outside the barrack door like blocks of wood, the screams from the execution wall, the blood-soaked snow – and spent his hours at Auschwitz nervously waiting for the Rat's wake-up call so he could escape to the stable where, hidden between the close walls of the stall, he felt safe and warm.

He spent his days feeding Midnight and grooming his winter coat, but mostly he talked to him. He told him about the farmhouse at Gregor Lane and his sister's favourite hiding spot, behind the woodpile in the shed. He told him about his father's rickety milk cart loaded with ice blocks to cool the milk and the day the soldier came for Sari's foal.

"I still remember his face," Alexander said as he worked to untangle Midnight's tail. "It was pockmarked. He wasn't much older than me. He said the army needed our horses. My mother said we couldn't run the farm without them. She argued with him until he pulled out his gun, then she sent me the stable to get them. She told him we had four he could use." Alexander stopped brushing. "We had five horses: the plough horse, the mare who pulled the milk cart, the Arabian my father had bought to help herd the cattle, Paprika and Sari. Paprika was Sari's foal. She was a yearling, just one and a half years old and not yet broken in. The army couldn't use her." Alexander looked at Midnight. "I had to give the soldier four horses," he sighed, "I wasn't going to give them my favourite, so I locked Sari into her stall and gave them Paprika."

Alexander counted down the days, carving their passing into his wooden bunk with the sharpened tip of his spoon. He figured it was the middle of January when the Rat met the Horse Platoon at the barrack door.

"I have an announcement," he shouted, driving the men inside the barrack. The other barrack inmates, the corpse collectors, tailors, machinists and welders were sitting on their bunks, waiting.

"We're being evacuated tomorrow," he said, the news twisting his mouth. The barrack erupted.

Men jumped from their bunks and leaped upon the barrack boss, pelting him with questions. Where were they going? Would they be fed? How long would the march last? Where would they sleep?

"Stand back!" He flicked his whip. "All you need to know is that tonight was the last roll-call. Tomorrow we march out." The men's eyes widened. "We leave after dark. Only the sick will remain in the infirmary and" – he scanned the room and caught Isidor's eye – "the Horse Platoon. You'll stay for as long as you're needed. Once your officers leave with their horses, there'll be no need for you to stay ..."

... *alive*, Alexander thought, finishing the Rat's sentence.

The Rat turned to the whispering men beside him and clubbed the nearest man on the head with the handle of his whip. The whispering stopped. "I don't know how long we'll be walking, or where we're headed, so don't ask me." He swung open the door and bent over the pile of dead heaped on the snow. "Now someone get over here and help me undress these bodies. Once I'm good and warm," he said, grabbing a dead man's coat, "you can fight over what's left."

Alexander climbed onto his bunk and looped his arms around his knees.

"It's a death sentence." A man three bunks down buried his head in his hands.

"I haven't fought to stay alive for two years to die now," another voice joined the chorus of panic. One of the tailors ripped a sheet in half and took a needle from his coat pocket while another draped a blanket around his shoulders, securing it at the waist with a piece of fraying rope. "Got to stay warm," they whispered to each other, packing mattress stuffing into their coats.

"You need those boots?" The boy on the bunk next to Alexander blinked nervously. "I can trade you a coat for them. A coat and a hat."

Alexander shook his head, pulled a carrot from his sock and bit into it. With or without boots, the boy wasn't going to survive the march. Not in the snow. Not without food or shelter.

Maybe that was the plan. Alexander swallowed the stump of the carrot. *I've been stupid*, he thought. *Stupid to underestimate the SS. To imagine they'd put down their guns and admit defeat. To expect they'd hand us over and leave Hitler's job undone.*

Isidor climbed onto his bunk. "I've heard the guards talking," he whispered to Alexander. "They have orders to liquidate whoever's left in the camp. In a couple of days this place will be a graveyard.

I'm not joining the march. And I'm sure as hell not staying here."

"So what do we do?" Alexander turned to face him.

"The only thing we *can* do. We get on our horses and get the hell out of here."

Alexander shook his head. "The guards have guns. They'll stop us."

"The guards don't care any more. They know it's over. They're just trying to work out how they can survive this. I only need to buy off the two in the yard. A few bottles of vodka, a promise to put in a good word for them with the Russians..."

Alexander pulled himself up to rest on an elbow. "A bottle of vodka's not a guarantee."

"You're right," Isidor conceded. "But if we do nothing, we're as good as dead."

"Maybe." Alexander shrugged. He thought of all the times Midnight had allowed him to steal food from his bucket. The horse had kept him warm on the coldest of days and nudged him awake when he fell asleep on the job. Midnight had done everything the commander – and Alexander – had asked of him so that neither of them would suffer at the hands of the commander's whip. He couldn't do it. Couldn't ride into a forest that might be teeming with SS and risk Midnight's life. Not after the horse had saved his.

He watched them leave. Watched them march through the front gate and head west: thousands of men, women and children, with blankets thrown over their shoulders and torn sheets wrapped around their arms and legs to stave off the cold. Colourless, caved-in faces, pouchy eyes and thin skin. He watched them spill out onto the snow, one by one, until there was just the Horse Platoon and the guards left to wander the camp and wait.

Forty officers came to the stable for their horses that morning. And forty stablehands waited anxiously for their horses to be returned at the end of the day. Twenty-seven horses came back.

"Your officers have left," the kapo told the thirteen frightened inmates whose horses weren't returned to them. "Your job is over. You won't be returning to Auschwitz tonight. You are joining the march."

They hadn't prepared for a hike. Their pockets were empty and their necks bare.

"I haven't eaten," one of the boys cried as a guard tore him from the platoon and ordered him to fall into line.

"I'm not ready," another boy begged the kapo. "You said we'd have a few days."

The kapo shrugged and the guard aimed his gun. One of the boys had stepped out of line. The guard spat a bullet into the snow and another into the boy's heel. Blood leaked onto the snow from his black boot.

"*Marsch!*" The guard shoved the boy forwards.

The kapo yelled at the remaining stablehands to feed and water their horses, slowing to walk beside Isidor as they neared the trough. Alexander saw Isidor reach into his pocket, pull out a package and hand it to the kapo.

"Your officer is listed to leave in two days. It'll be a long hike. Feed your horse up. You don't want him getting hungry and weak," Alexander overheard him say, a hint wedged between the words. "Make sure he is dressed warm." The kapo glanced down at Isidor's shoes which were coming away at the heel. "And see to his shoes."

The kapo left and Isidor followed Alexander into the feed room and shut the door behind them. "I'm escaping tomorrow, soon as I get to the stable. My officer has been ordered to march out in two days." He grabbed a carrot and slipped it under his cap. Alexander's head started to pound.

"So you're not going to join the march?"

Isidor shook his head and stuffed an apple down his trousers.

"There's only one guard left in the yard. I know him, he likes his drink. He'll look the other way for a bottle of vodka. You can join me."

Alexander ignored the invitation. "I want to give you something," he said instead, pulling Isidor from the feed room to the mare's stable. "I should have told you about it earlier." He reddened. He took a milk pail from the shelf. "I've been milking her," he said, shooing the foal from her mother. "I didn't tell anyone because I was worried she'd dry up if she was milked too often." He pulled on the mare's teat. "It was selfish. I'm sorry." His voice trailed away. He finished milking, left the pail for Isidor and hurried to Midnight's stall.

"I don't want to say goodbye to him." He wrapped his arms around the horse's neck and touched his cheek to Midnight's. "Or to you. You're the only friends I've got." *Friends.* The thought of the word swelled to fill the stall. Alexander sifted through his memories for the last time he'd done something to benefit someone other than himself. It had been a while. It was his own fault. He'd convinced himself that the only way to survive the camp was to be as cold and hard as the men who'd locked him up. To give nothing out and let no one in. All those months batting away his feelings hadn't made him into a fortress. It had whittled him away. He dragged his fingers through Midnight's mane. It had taken a horse to teach him how to be human. A horse as scared and lost as he was. Alexander pulled his hands from Midnight's mane and stroked his nose.

"You let yourself be vulnerable. That takes a lot of strength." *To need people. To help them. And accept their help in return.* "The commander will come for you soon." Alexander wiped his eyes with the back of his hand. "You're finally getting out of here." Midnight nudged Alexander with his nose. "It's OK. I'm going too," he said, letting the horse lick his tears. "The Russians are close, so this will all be over soon and we'll make it back home, both of us. And when we do," he said, kneading his hope into certainty, "someone will be there, waiting for us. You'll see. "

The barrack was empty when Alexander returned to camp. He sat on the steps in the staggering cold with a blanket wrapped around his legs, watching Isidor and the remaining stablehands search the camp for food.

"They're not giving us any more meals," the Rat said. He took a wilted cabbage leaf from his pocket and stuffed it into his mouth. "You'll have to fend for yourself."

Alexander stepped onto the snow and snapped an icicle from the roof. The quiet should have been comforting. The band had packed away their instruments and the gallows had been pulled down. The roll-call square was silent and the barracks emptied. The camp had been scraped clean and Alexander felt hollow.

He heard a throaty rumble and dived backwards through the door as an aeroplane screamed overhead, filling the sky with flames. He thought about joining Isidor, if not on horseback, then by foot, but there were still guards at the gate, maybe more in the forest. And even if they made it past the guards, they wouldn't survive a night in the snow.

He climbed onto his bunk. He hadn't slept on his back for seven months, hadn't drifted off to sleep without someone's stinking body touching his. Now the barrack was almost empty. He had a bed to himself, and still, he couldn't sleep.

"We're marching out." Isidor stood at the foot of Alexander's bunk the next morning. It was still dark outside, but the Rat was pulling men from their bunks and a guard stood at the open door of the barrack, yelling at them to hurry. "This morning," Isidor said, his face white as chalk. Alexander rubbed the sleep from his eyes and sat up.

"Now? From here?" his voice splintered. He hadn't said goodbye to Midnight.

Isidor nodded. He retrieved a crumbling sugar cube from under his mattress and slipped it into his cap.

"You're not coming with us," he said, staring up at Alexander. "The commander's here, so you still have a job." He lifted his pillow and took the apple core that was under it. "But he won't stick around." He glanced at the guard, waiting by the door to march the men out. "You should leave today. I've already paid off the guard at the stable. Take the commander's horse and get the hell out of there." He gripped Alexander's arm. "I don't want to see you on that march."

"Can't you buy an extra day from the guards or the kapo?" Alexander panicked. "You've got a friend at the infirmary. He'll say you're unwell."

"I gave the stable guard my last pack of cigarettes. I've got nothing left to give, so I've got no friends."

"You've got *me*," Alexander said, feeling punctured.

"I thought you didn't *want* friends."

"I didn't," Alexander said. "You wore me down." He extended his hand and Isidor took it. "The Russians are close," Alexander tried to sound convincing, "they'll stop the march."

Isidor nodded, pulled his bedsheet from his mattress and tore it to strips, winding a band of fabric around his chest and each of his arms. He wound the final strip around his left shoe where the sole came away at the heel.

Alexander attempted a smile. "Six Gregor Lane, Košice. Remember it. It's my address. After we both get out of here, I expect you to visit."

"Horse Platoon, march out!" A second guard stood at the door, his beard covered in ice.

"Six Gregor Lane." Isidor stood up, pulled his coat on and walked towards the door, the fabric around his battered left shoe unravelling as he walked.

"Isidor, wait!" Alexander kicked off one boot, then the other. He wasn't about to lose his new friend. His only friend. "Your shoes are falling apart. They won't last in the snow. You don't have time to fix them. *I* do." He scooped the boots from the floor and pressed them to Isidor's chest. "Take mine. I'll wear yours."

Chapter 22

Alexander stood at the main gate and watched Isidor disappear into the fog.

"Six Gregor Lane," he said quietly into the swirling snow. "And bring my father's boots. He'll want them back."

The Rat handed Alexander over to the kapo and the two of them marched to the stable, escorted by a guard. Alexander knew he was lucky to have been spared. Lucky to have another few hours of shelter, another swipe at the food bins. Lucky to have Midnight's protection. At least for now. He knew *now* wouldn't last. The commander would escape before the Russian tanks arrived and then he'd be out there too, dragging his feet through the snow to God knows where.

"The commander hasn't said whether he'll be riding today." The kapo swung the stable door open and marched past a grim-faced guard. Alexander hurried after him, past the quiet kitchen and the empty feed room. The stalls were deserted, the hooks on the shelves stripped of saddles and reins. Alexander stopped outside Chestnut's empty stall and the kapo shook his head. "They let him loose in the forest last night. The foal too."

"And the mare?" Alexander asked, remembering finding his own mother at the fence dividing the women's camp from the men's on his third day in Birkenau, and how it felt having her ripped away from him, a second time.

"They took the mare with them."

Alexander tore into Midnight's stall and wrapped his arms around the stallion. "Want to go riding?" he asked, strapping a saddle to Midnight's back. Midnight's ears pricked up and he shifted towards the door. "Not out there. In here, with me." He knew it was foolish, but he also knew he might never ride again and he wanted to feel a horse under him, one last time. Wanted to wrap his hands around the reins and press his heels into Midnight's sides and pretend just for a moment that he was a boy on a horse.

He fastened the girth and slipped the bit into Midnight's wet mouth.

"Where should we go?" he said, climbing onto the horse's back and closing his eyes. Midnight nickered gently and shifted his feet, and Alexander heard the pressing of hooves against grass, then the wind in the trees. He tightened his hands around the reins, sunk his heels into the stirrups and lifted himself to stand. He felt the sun on his face, saw the grassy acres in front of them, then the path to Gregor Lane. He sped up to a gallop, his legs absorbing every bump in the road, every pothole and rock. His mother was at the farmhouse gate, wiping her hands on her apron and Lili was beside her, calling Alexander to come home.

Home ... I have to get home! He slid from the horse, grabbed a blanket from the straw and draped it over his shoulders, fixing it at the waist with a rope. He filled his pockets with sugar cubes and his socks with oats scraped from the feed bins. "They could take me today," he said. He pulled Isidor's shoes from his feet and ran to the farrier's shed. He turned Isidor's left shoe over, pulled a hammer from the workbench and pounded a dozen nails into the sole, filing the edges with the farrier's rasp, before returning to feed Midnight.

"They're setting fire to the warehouses and blowing up the barracks. I don't want to go back to camp," Alexander said, pressing his cheek to Midnight's neck. "Isidor said we should escape, but you're better off with the commander," he told the horse. "You'll be safe with him."

When the sky turned black, the kapo rapped at the door. Alexander pulled Midnight towards him, pressed his forehead to Midnight's white blaze and said goodbye.

"We're going back to camp." The kapo dipped his voice. "Maybe they'll come tonight." His voice rippled with hope. He didn't say who he hoped would come to Auschwitz, but he didn't need to. Alexander looked up at the bleeding sky. *Please hurry*, he begged the Russians. *We haven't got long.*

The Rat was gone by the time Alexander returned to his barrack. Sitting alone in the dark on the edge of his bunk, Alexander wondered whether Midnight could smell the flames licking the barrack next door or hear the walls of the warehouses collapsing. His stomach grumbled but he didn't want to empty his pockets or shake out his socks; he needed the food for the march. He climbed off his bunk and combed the floor on his hands and knees for a heel of bread or a corner of cheese. He dragged the mattresses from their planks and swept his fingers over the splintering boards, crawling under the lowest tier of bunks to feel for crumbs in the dark, but the floor was licked clean. He stood at the door to the Rat's bedroom and slowly pushed it open. He'd imagined a lamp on a table, a desk and a chair, clean sheets and a pillow. It was a room, that was true, with four walls and a door, a bed and a nightstand, but there was nothing else to distinguish it from the squalor of the barrack. Alexander lifted the mattress from the bed and tipped the nightstand upside down but the Rat had left nothing behind.

An old man slipped between the burned-out barracks calling for his son. Alexander wiped an arc across the frosted window pane with his sleeve and watched the old man, wishing he could sneak out in search of his mother. The kapo had told him that his barrack was protected and that if he wandered outside alone, he took his life in his own hands. *I'd leave here if I could*, he told himself. *I'd check the women's barracks and the latrines. I'd search the kitchen and the infirmary.* Isidor had told him that the infirmary smelled like death, that the patients were pin-thin and that if they took too long to die, the SS doctors injected them with phenol to speed things up.

He pressed his nose to the window and stared out at the barracks. A guard had lit a fire on the steps of block fourteen and was hurling a box of papers into the flames. An officer swept past him, pulling on a blue-and-white jacket. He had a pen in his hand and was scratching something onto the skin of his forearm.

"The Russians are coming. You won't get away with this," Alexander hissed at the darting shadows. He lay down on his bed but he couldn't sleep, not with the rumbling trucks and the spitting flames and the end of the war hurtling towards him. He climbed from his bunk, collected some snow from the barrack roof for breakfast and waited for the kapo to collect him.

"The commander will be in early," the kapo said as they set off for the stable.

Alexander opened his mouth. "Is he leaving?"

"I don't know." The kapo chewed on a fingernail. "He hasn't said where he's going."

They marched in silence, stepping into the yard as the dark of night left the sky. The commander appeared at the stall door moments later, looked in on his horse, then stalked off. Alexander was left alone with the horse, to worry over his fate.

They spent three days in the stable together, waiting for the commander to return or for the war to end. The kapo waited with them. Alexander prepared Midnight every morning and stripped his tack every night before returning to the barrack.

"They've blown up the last of the crematoria and set fire to the storage barracks," the kapo said one morning as they sat in the feed room between the empty bins. "They're destroying the evidence. It's over. You'll be home soon."

But it wasn't. There was still the clawing hunger and the cold. There were still guards with guns. The commander could turn up tomorrow and order them both onto the march. Alexander scooped the last scraps from a feed bin and added it to his stockpile. Since the feed deliveries had tapered off, his pile had dwindled until all that was left was a handful of grain and a few potatoes he'd dug up. He picked a bruised one from the pile and shared it with Midnight.

"Antreten! Alles Raus! Schnell! Schnell!"

Alexander heard a guard's heavy footsteps coming towards him.

"Get out of bed!" the man yelled, shoving the butt of his rifle into Alexander's back.

"But I look after the commander's horse." Alexander's face crumpled. "They'll be expecting me at the stable."

"Not any more you don't," the guard flared. "You're done." He wrapped his fingers around Alexander's collar and dragged him from his bed.

"That can't be," Alexander stammered, reaching for his shoes. "The commander needs someone to saddle his horse." The guard's face twisted in anger.

"The commander's gone." His words were sharp as flint. "Now get out!"

By the time Alexander joined the march, the snow was stained red. The road Isidor had travelled before him was littered with bodies. Alexander had seen death, but never like this – bodies slumped on top of each other in ditches, their shirts matted with blood.

Alexander hadn't been old enough to attend his grandfather's funeral but he remembered crouching behind the bushes at the cemetery and seeing his grandfather's stiff body wrapped in cloth. He remembered his *Zaida* being lowered into the ground and the prayer his father had whispered as he bent over the grave. Alexander's lips formed words, Hebrew words: *Yitgaddal veyitquaddash shmeh rabba…*

He lifted his wet shoes from the snow and pushed his tired legs forwards. There was no use trying to escape. The few who had tried had been set upon by dogs. He hoped Isidor hadn't tried to slip from the line. He dragged his eyes from the slumped bodies, saw the kapo marching ahead of him and remembered the man's last words: you'll be home soon. *Home*, he said to himself. *If I can just get home.*

He dug his hand into his pocket, pulled a sugar cube from the sticky seam and slid it into his mouth.

When the moon was high the men stopped for the night. Alexander recognized a few of the men – they were engineers, kitchen hands and clerical workers – men who had been useful to the SS and had been spared, until now. The kapo found Alexander and sunk into the snow beside him, but neither of them spoke. Alexander bit his lips to stop them from freezing. He sat in the cold snow and gulped down his fear. It was still dark when the guards ordered them to keep marching and only half the men rose.

"Alles Raus!"

Alexander pushed his hunger aside and rose on shaky legs.

"Vorwärts Marsch! Eins, zwei…"

Alexander looked up and saw the commander's black shadow first, then four perfect white socks. *Midnight!* His heart flailed in his chest. *Midnight!* His lips parted, but no sound came out.

"Eins, zwei!"

The commander steered his horse past Alexander, continued a few metres, then pulled on the reins and circled back up the line, looking down at the ragged men as he passed them, his face fierce, as if on a hunt.

"Eins, zwei!"

The commander slowed the horse to a walk. They were two rows from Alexander. Close enough for Alexander to see the white blaze between Midnight's eyes. Close enough to see the horse stop and raise his head.

Midnight planted his legs firmly in the snow. He pricked his ears forwards and lifted his nose to sniff the air. *He can smell me*, Alexander realized, feeling panicked and proud at the same time. The commander's mouth puckered. He urged Midnight to go but the horse wouldn't budge.

"*Gehen! Laufen!* Go!" The commander lifted his leather whip in the air. He brought the strap down on Midnight's back leg and the horse's wide eyes narrowed in pain. He snorted and threw his head from side to side, his black eyes searching the shadows for Alexander's outline, for the soft eyes and kind hands that went with the familiar smell.

Alexander touched his nose to his sleeve to smell the sweat — the scent — that tethered Midnight to the spot, cursing himself for putting the horse in danger. *I've got to get him to move before the commander strikes him on the head*, he thought. He tore through the column — taking his scent with him — shoving aside the women who walked in front of him and elbowing the men who blocked his path, while the commander slashed at the horse, his face purpling as he brought the crop down hard on Midnight's back and neck. *Come on boy, keep up with me, keep moving, don't stop.* Alexander glanced back at Midnight and saw the commander tug on the reins and the horse tuck his chin to his chest to fight off the bit.

The commander clenched the whip's heavy wooden handle. He brought the long leather strap crashing down on Midnight's head and when Midnight lifted it again Alexander could see the moon – and the horse's fear – reflected in his dark eyes. He couldn't just stand there and watch the commander lash Midnight's head. He remembered what he'd said to the horse the first day they met – *You're going to have to trust me; I'm all you've got.*

He knew what he had to do. Flinging himself into a deep drift, he burrowed into the wet snow to bury his scent. He scraped handfuls of snow over his chest and legs, until he couldn't feel his fingers or his toes. He hoped the guards hadn't seen him. He didn't want to die. *Not now, not after all I've been through. And so close to seeing my parents and climbing onto Sari's back.*

He closed his eyes and made himself as still as a corpse, so the guards would think him dead. He heard a dog bark and a guard hissing commands. Fear – and the shock of the cold — pumped through his body but he made his face blank. He heard the snap of leather and Midnight's frightened squeals. He felt the ground shift and the snow flurry around him as the column of inmates marched past. He heard a strangled cry, a distant gunshot, fewer footsteps, and then just the wind. *Go*, he begged Midnight. *Please go.*

He didn't know how long he lay in his icy bed with his teeth chattering and his eyes squeezed shut, but he didn't move until Midnight's shrieking subsided, and then found that he couldn't. He heard a triumphant cry and, lifting his eyes to the lightening sky saw, through the departing column of prisoners, the commander's black shadow move slowly away. He wanted to reach out and rub Midnight's neck and tell him he was a good boy. Instead he said goodbye, the words frozen in his throat.

The commander's outline became a black blot and then a speck. Alexander's head felt heavy and his body numb. The wind scattered his thoughts. He wasn't cold any more, just tired. So tired. His eyes fluttered closed. *Sleep, Alex, you're exhausted*, he heard his mother say. She cupped his face in her hands and lowered his head onto the snow. It was soft as a pillow. *You're tired, Alex, sleep*, she whispered, her warm hand on his cheek. Alexander let his shoulders sink into the soft snow and his muscles loosen. *I'll see you tomorrow*, she said, her warm breath on his skin. Then she turned down the lights and the room went dark.

Chapter 23

Alexander opened his eyes. He looked up, expecting to see sky, but saw, instead, the sloping wooden beams of a barn. He swept his hands over the hard dirt floor and tried to remember how he'd got there. Images of the night before skittered across his lids.

"Alexander!" The kapo hurried to kneel beside him, his face flush with relief. "You're awake!" He rocked back on his knees and helped Alexander sit up. "Here, have some water." He pushed a blackened tin mug into Alexander's hands and rummaged through the basket at his feet. Alexander dropped the mug and snatched a beet from the basket, sinking his teeth into the plump purple flesh.

"How long have I been sleeping? Where are we?" Sweet red juice dribbled down his chin.

"We're on a farm, just outside Katowice."

Alexander looked at the kapo blankly. "Whose

farm? How did we get here?" He swallowed the beet and grabbed another.

The corners of the kapo's mouth turned upwards and Alexander realized he'd never seen the man smile.

"We came by horse and cart. You've been sleeping for two days."

"And the march?" Alexander remembered the dogs and the guards and the bodies by the side of the road. "I was buried in the snow. How did you…"

"I saw you fall and bury yourself." The kapo pulled a radish from the basket and passed it to Alexander. "You wanted to escape."

Alexander didn't correct him.

"I thought you were crazy, burying yourself like that, but they marched right past you. No one pulled you from the ground or shot at you."

Alexander waited.

"So I did the same. I lay still until they were gone, then I crawled over and dug you out. I forced some snow into your mouth and went for help. This was the first place I found." The kapo bit into a carrot.

"How did I get here?" Alexander looked down at his waterlogged shoes.

"I convinced the farmer to pick you up with his cart."

"I don't remember climbing into a cart." Alexander searched his memory.

"You didn't." The kapo reddened. "I lifted you on."

"And the farmer?"

"He didn't want to take us in, but I told him the Russians were coming. Told him if he didn't help us, he'd be siding with the enemy."

"So we're safe here?" Alexander felt doubtful. "He won't turn us in?" Alexander took the bread the kapo offered him, tore it in half and slipped the larger half into his pocket.

"You don't need to save it." The kapo drew Alexander's hand from his pocket. "There's plenty to eat."

Alexander pulled a shovel from the wall and, clutching it like a weapon, crept to the barn door. "Maybe we should go. We don't know this man. He could be alerting the Nazis right now."

"Alex," the kapo said softly. "You can leave whenever you want. The Russians have stormed Auschwitz. You're free."

The shovel slipped from Alexander's hand and clattered to the floor.

"You can go home, Alex." The kapo smiled. "We can both go home."

* * *

Alexander stood in the middle of Gregor Lane under his dripping cap, his knees trembling. He'd swung the gate open to number 6 more times than he could remember, and yet he was scared. He'd got through the war by telling himself his parents would be waiting for him. But what if they weren't? What if he walked down the rutted path to his home and found it empty? He'd dreamed of this street, of the fields that stretched out to forever and the endless sky. Alexander lifted his eyes to the gabled house, and it was just as he remembered it, just as he'd hoped. He sensed his family's footsteps nearby, their dark silhouettes and the echo of their voices. He pushed the gate open and stepped into the sinking mud. *I'm home.* He smiled, then said it out loud, "I'm home."

He ran across the soggy front lawn, past the pole for tethering horses and the towering birch tree with its empty swing, until he reached the front door. He stepped inside, kicking Isidor's muddy shoes from his feet. The house was just as he'd left it the night the Hungarian police ordered his family into the ghetto: the pots hanging from hooks on the wall, the ladles beside them, his mother's lace tablecloth on the dining table, four chairs clustered around it and Spitz's small, round bowl in a corner on the floor. Alexander listened for the patter of dog feet but the house was silent. The clock on the wall had stopped at one fifty-two, its thin black hands raised in surrender.

Alexander walked along the quiet corridor and peered into each of the rooms. He opened the cupboards and the drawers and pulled back the drapes, searching for spaces where a father might be or a mother might hide, but the house was empty. He tiptoed into Lili's room and stood at the end of her bed, afraid to wake her ghost. Her soft toys lay in a jumble on her bed, and on her wooden dresser, the jewellery box he'd made her in carpentry class lay open, its drawers emptied. He remembered clamping his hand over her mouth the night the police tore through her room, and how she'd howled when she discovered her jewellery box upside down on the floor. The police left that night with Lili's silver bangle, his mother's pearl earrings, his father's camera and their sewing machine. *Be happy they're taking things, not people*, his mother had whispered into Lili's hair. *You can always get a new bracelet. You can't get a new brother.*

Alexander bent in half and wept into his cupped hands.

He wasn't angry any more. He wasn't angry at

Lili for dying or angry with himself for letting her. He just missed her. "I miss you," he cried. "I miss you lying on my bed with your nose in one of my books. I miss you tugging at my sleeve to come push you on the swing. I miss your piano recitals and the endless games of hide-and-seek. I miss the sound of your spoon scraping the last of the porridge from your bowl." Alexander closed his eyes and tried to picture his sister's face, tried to recall her freckles and the dimples either side of her mouth. He'd fought so hard not to think of her, fearing her face would bring him undone, not realising, as he did now, that the memories might warm him.

The room was too quiet and he felt himself drifting away, untethered from his family. "I'm alone," he said, fighting the silence. He thought he heard the fireplace sputter and ran to the kitchen, his heart thumping, but the room was empty and the brick pit dark. He pulled on Isidor's battered shoes then froze, hunched over the laces. A sound slipped through the walls: a muffled padding then the sound of running water. *It's not in my head.* Alexander's eyes widened. *It's real. And it's coming from outside.* "Mother?" he called, hope galloping towards him. He flung the back door open and stumbled to the barn, running between the stalls to find, in the very last stall, a woman smaller than his mother, older too, with thinner skin and bloodshot eyes.

The woman stared up at him. "Alex?"

Alexander stared into the woman's round eyes.

"Alex. You're alive?" Her rake fell to the ground. "You're alive!" she shouted, taking his hands in hers and propelling him backwards to get a better look.

"Mother?"

The woman smiled.

"Mother, is it really you?" The woman's front teeth were chipped, but she had his mother's pale lips and her smile, like a crescent moon. Alexander's stomach turned inside out.

"You came back." She squeezed his hands. "I knew you would."

He had a mountain of questions for her but she didn't want to talk about the camp, it hurt too much. "We're together and that's all that matters," she said, drawing him into her. "You're so thin. Are you hungry?"

Alexander shook his head. He hadn't eaten for hours but he didn't want to let her go, couldn't let her walk away, even if it were only to leave the barn. He wanted to ask about his father but he didn't know how. His mother was so brittle; he didn't want her to break. They stood, collapsed into each other, the silence loud between them, until, finally, it was too much for him and he had to know.

"Tell me about Father," he said, pulling away to look at her.

"He hasn't come back yet," she said. "But he will." Her eyes were dry, her lips set tight. "You've travelled a long way." She reached for the rake and set it against a wall. "You must be exhausted, come inside. I'll fix you something to eat." She didn't want him to ask about his father or Lili. She wanted to feed him and pretend they were still a family, and do what she could to make him whole. She could prepare him a meal. She couldn't bring back his sister.

Alexander nodded. "I will," he said. "I'll be there in a moment."

His mother watched him scan the empty stalls, looking for Sari. "Of course," she whispered, resting a hand on his cheek. "Come when you're ready."

Alexander padded through the empty barn to Sari's stall, wondering who his neighbour had sold her to. He scooped a handful of straw from the ground and held it to his nose. He could still smell her, still make out the outline of her sleeping body on the straw. He wet his lips, stuck two fingers into his mouth and whistled, just for the hell of it. Just to remember how it felt to call a horse and have it come.

He imagined hooves churning through the muddy ground, the clink of metal stirrups and the slapping sound of leather. He felt the ground shudder and realized it wasn't his imagination, the sound and movement were real.

"Whoa! Slow down girl!"

Alexander swung around to face the barn door. He didn't recognize his neighbour's voice until he saw Radomir Hudak run through the door clutching Sari's reins, his heels fighting the dirt in a vain attempt to stop her.

Alexander's mouth dropped open as Sari flew through the stable, dragging Radomir after her.

"Sari!" Alexander found his voice. The mare ground to a halt with her ears pricked forwards and her tail held high.

"You're still here!" He took a step forwards and Sari walked towards him.

"Alex, it's good to see you!" Radomir extended his hand. Alexander didn't take it. He stood nose to nose with his horse and swept his hand over her dripping neck. She sniffed his shoes, then his pants, lifted her wet nose to his chest and leaned into him.

"Sari," he croaked, looking into the horse's brown eyes. He swept the raindrops from her forelock and ran his fingers through her wet mane. Sari nickered gently and hung her head over his shoulder.

"She missed you." Radomir lifted the saddle from Sari's back and pulled the bit from her mouth. Alexander watched him tend to the mare as if she was his own, and realized, she was. His father had signed the farm over to the Hudaks when the government decreed that Jews couldn't own property. The farmhouse, the ten acres, and every animal on it was his. Alexander's insides felt bruised.

"Radomir, you're back." Alexander's mother slipped into the barn, carrying a plate of biscuits. Alexander took the plate from her and set it on a stool, away from their thieving neighbour. His mother's face flushed.

"Alex!" she scolded.

"It's OK, Mrs Altmann," Radomir said, passing her the lead rope. "I was leaving anyway. You have a lot to catch up on."

Alexander bristled. *You might own the farm*, he wanted to shout at the pink-cheeked farmer, *but she doesn't work for you. And neither do I.*

"Thank you, Radomir." His mother half bowed and Alexander felt a burning in the pit of his stomach. "You don't know how much it means," she continued, "to have a home to come back to. To be here when my husband walks through the gate." She turned from Radomir to look at her son. "Radomir signed the papers last week. The farm is ours again."

Alexander's mouth fell open.

"It was never mine to keep." Radomir blushed. "It's yours. It always was."

He bowed to Alexander's mother, nodded to Alexander, and left.

"The farm is ours? He can't take it off us?" Alexander waited for the door to swing closed. "It's in your name?"

"He can't take it from us," Alexander's mother said, taking her son's hands in hers. "But the papers aren't in my name. Not any more." She handed Alexander Sari's rope, the hint of a smile on her lips. "It's yours now. Six Gregor Lane belongs to you."

The table was set with his mother's best silver.

"Is Radomir joining us?" Alexander asked when he saw the table was set for three. His mother shook her head and pulled an apron from the cupboard. It was Lili's, a red-and-white checked apron with an embroidered hem.

"Mother, Lili's not coming back." Alexander's voice broke.

"I know," his mother answered, tying the apron around her waist. "I like to wear it when I cook. It feels like she's with me in the kitchen." She spooned soup into a bowl. "The spare table setting is for your father."

They broke bread and ate two bowls of cauliflower soup and a plate of stuffed cabbages swimming in sauce. Alexander licked the plate clean and asked for another.

"I want to show you something," his mother said, as he mopped up the last of the sauce with a slab of bread. She opened the pantry door, scraped a chair from the table and climbed onto it, reaching up to the highest shelf to pull a battered cardboard box from behind a fruit bowl.

"I hid a few things before we left for the ghetto," she said, peeling the lid open, and Alexander remembered waking the night after the police stole Lili's bracelet to find his mother in his room, holding a torch. She'd put a finger to her lips and told him to go back to sleep.

"I kept Rabbit for Lili." His mother pulled a cloth rabbit from the box. "And my wedding ring." Her voice trailed away. She pulled a gold band from its velvet bag and slipped it onto her finger. "It's too big," she said, surprised by her thin fingers. She slipped the ring back into its pouch. "We kept your father's prayer book too, and a set of candlesticks."

She rummaged through the box. "And this," she said pulling a splintered wooden sign from the battered carton.

The Galloping Stallion Equestrian Park. Alexander read the letters carved into the wood. It seemed like a lifetime ago.

He took the sign from his mother and tucked it under his arm.

"And one last thing." His mother pulled a wad of blue banknotes from the leather pouch. "It's not a lot, but it's a start, enough to buy a few foals to train, and make a reputation for yourself." Tears hung on her lids. "They shaved your head and stole your name but you're still Alexander Altmann." His mother pressed the notes into his hand. "You're still entitled to the same dreams."

Alexander kissed his mother's cheek. "You were here waiting for me, so they're coming true already." He tucked the money she had given him into the pocket of Lili's apron. "Can you keep it for me, until I'm ready?" Alexander's mother nodded and took his hands in hers. He looked down at her crepe paper hands, mottled with age, and then at his own, surprised by the smooth skin. His palms were unpuckered, the scars faded. No longer an angry red, they were now a pale pink.

Alexander thanked his mother for lunch and headed back to the barn. Sari was waiting for him in her stall, her head cocked towards the barn door.

"How about a ride?" he said, pulling a saddle from the straw. Sari nickered and dipped her head for the bridle. Alexander tightened the girth and led her outside, grabbing the reins in one hand and a handful of mane in the other. He slid his foot into the stirrup, swung his leg over Sari's back and landed in the seat. He didn't hunch over and make himself small or look around to see who might be watching. He sat up tall and asked Sari to go. She took off through the yard, at the touch of his heels and stopped at the front gate.

"Spitz!" Alexander cried, when he saw his dog digging at the fence. He leaped from Sari's back to scoop the dog from the ground, rubbing his belly and his back before lowering him to the ground.

"Find your ball. When I get back we'll play catch." He climbed back onto the horse and took off at a trot. Sari bounced along the rutted dirt road and slid into a canter, passing farmers at work tilling the fields and women bent over their baskets, pulling vegetables from the soil. Alexander's neighbours stared at him wide-eyed, as if seeing a ghost.

He ran his hands over Sari's windswept mane and

coaxed her into a gallop. Sari knew where to go without being asked. She flew down Gregor Lane and cut through the woods, scaring the birds into the trees.

"Whoa." Alexander closed his fingers around the reins and brought the mare to a stop outside an empty paddock, the paddock he'd visited more than a dozen times with Anton.

He hopped off the horse, pulled a hunting knife from Sari's saddlebag and, balancing the sign his mother had saved for him on a fence post, scratched Anton's name from the wood and carved his friend's name in its place – a boy who shared the same dreams he had, and the same demons.

He hammered the sign to the gate and stepped back to admire his handiwork. The black stallion he'd etched into the wood when he was twelve reared up over the capital letters.

"The Galloping Stallion Equestrian Park," Alexander read the words out loud. *"Proprietors: Alexander Altmann and Isidor Finkler."*

He climbed onto Sari's back and pointed to a patch of dirt.

"The training arena will be over there," he said, "and just beyond it," he paused, pointing to a stretch of grass, "will be the stables." Alexander closed his eyes and pictured the stalls filled with horses: black, white and burnished bay. And in the very last stall, next to Sari's, a black stallion with a white blaze between his eyes and four perfect white socks.

Author's note

Every book has a backstory. *Alexander Altmann A10567* began in 2012 in a lecture hall at the Jewish Holocaust Centre in Melbourne. At the conclusion of the lecture an elderly man raised his hand and asked whether the speaker had ever met a kind German. He wore a short-sleeve shirt; the number the SS had given him a black stain across the white skin of his forearm. He answered before the speaker had a chance to respond. "Because *I* have," he whispered.

I found him after the lecture and introduced myself. I asked if he wouldn't mind meeting me the next day. I wanted to hear his story. I'd just finished writing *The Wrong Boy*, a story about Hanna, a Jewish girl in Auschwitz who befriends the son of the camp commandant. I wanted the boy – Karl – to be nothing like his father. I made him kind and I let him sneak her food. I let them fall in love. I knew it was unlikely that the son of a high-ranking Nazi would defy his father in this way, but I wanted it to be possible.

"I tell my story every day at the Holocaust museum downstairs," the old man said. "Come see me tomorrow."

His name was Fred. He'd grown up on a farm and spent his days riding horses, so when the Nazis asked for inmates to work in the SS stables, Fred put up his hand. He joined Auschwitz's elite Horse Commando and, sometimes when he took the SS officers' children on pony rides, the men would give him cigarettes which he could trade for food.

"Were *they* the kind Germans you spoke of?" I asked.

He shook his head. "The commander of the platoon drove me to his house to chop wood one morning and left me in the kitchen with his wife. She poured me coffee and fed me cake." He smiled. "She asked for my name. My name," he repeated. "She used my name."

The commander had beaten Fred black and blue. He'd whipped most of the men in the platoon at one time or another, but the man's wife had fed him cake and given him back his name.

Alexander Altmann A10567 is inspired by the story Fred Steiner told me in the months that followed. Much of what happens to Alexander, happened to

Fred. Some of it I made up. Fred has no scars on his palms. He didn't beat down his feelings or close himself off from the other men in the platoon and he never lost hope.

He was one of the lucky ones. He survived the war and made a new life in Australia. He married a French woman and had three children. He was finally safe, but he didn't sleep well. The nightmares stopped only when he became a guide at the Holocaust museum and started talking about his experience.

In 1997 Fred Steiner returned to Auschwitz with his son's class. Beside his name in the visitor's book, he wrote: *I was here as a slave. Today I'm here with my family and a class of Jewish schoolchildren. I have won.*

Fred is still telling people about his time in Auschwitz. He continues to work as a guide at the Holocaust museum because it keeps the nightmares at bay and because he knows that talking about the Holocaust is the best way to stop it from happening again.

Having you read this book and learn something of his life, and the Holocaust, is another small win.

Acknowledgements

My grateful thanks to Walker Books Australia for allowing me to return to my desk to write another story. And to Maryann Ballantyne for asking the right questions and allowing me the time to find the answers. Thanks also to Mary Verney for her careful copyedit, Sue Whiting for her meticulous proofreading and Sue Hampel for her expert advice.

I'm indebted to my writing group, Ilka Tampke, Michelle Deans, Brooke Maggs, Richard Holt, Carla Fedi and Melinda Dundas for always telling me the truth. And to my husband Shaun, who let me disappear for hours at a time, and our three beautiful children, Josh, Tanya and Remy, for their patience and encouragement.

And finally, to Fred Steiner, for telling me his story and allowing me to re-imagine it.

SUZY ZAIL was born in Melbourne, where she studied law and worked as a solicitor. She has written for magazines and newspapers and is the author of award-winning children's books published in Australia, Canada and the United States. She has written a number of books for adults, including *The Tattooed Flower*, an account of how her father survived the Holocaust. *The Wrong Boy*, her first work of fiction for young adults, was shortlisted for Book of the Year in the Older Readers category at the 2013 Children's Book Council of Australia Awards.

Hanna Mendel was going to be a famous pianist.
But the Nazis had another plan.
Thrown into Auschwitz, she plays piano
for a camp commandant and wears
a dead girl's dress pinned with a yellow star.
And she is falling in love — with the wrong boy.

*"Brilliant, important and absolutely heartbreaking.
It's one of the best fictional accounts of the Holocaust I've read...
For anyone who's read and enjoyed*
The Book Thief, The Boy in the Striped Pyjamas *and*
Between Shades of Gray." —Wondrous Reads

During the round-up of Jews in Paris in July 1942,
ten-year-old Jonas Alber is whisked away to the home
of an elderly music professor to live in hiding.
He reads about his favourite subjects – sharks, salmon,
albatrosses – and writes about his family, and his friends at
the circus. Increasingly he worries about his younger sister,
and one day dares to step outside to find her.

*"Perfect for any historical YA fan. And a must for those who
enjoy an uplifting tale of hope, family and friendship."*
—snugglingonthesofa.com